Catcher, Lover, Spy

By: David W. Huffstetler

Inspired by the Life of Moe Berg

Becher House Publishing

Chapter One

Moe Berg had never murdered anyone, and the prospect gnawed at him, as he paced the snow-covered sidewalk in front of the lecture hall in Zurich. And, he argued with himself. *You can't just shoot a man down in cold blood. But, if he perfects the bomb, millions could die. It's only right for one to die to save many. It's murder, Moe. No, there's no such thing as murder in war.* There was no winning the argument. There was only duty, and the time for debate was over.

He stepped before a broad soldier clad in a dark, gray uniform, highlighted by a swastika sewn into a red arm band. Berg presented his identification, and the soldier barked, "What is your business here?"

Moe stood three inches taller than the corporal, but he lowered his gaze and answered in his best German, "I am a physics student at the University of Basel, come to hear Doctor Heisenberg's lecture. I have a letter of introduction from the university."

"Let me see it." He drew an envelope from his coat pocket and handed it to the soldier. "Yes, this seems to be in order, but you strike me as too old for a student."

Berg forced a wry grin. "My wife says that too." The air grew heavy, as he waited for an answer. Would he have to shoot this soldier? No, then he'd never get to Heisenberg. Slip in the back? Impossible with guards at every door. Could the future of the war rest in the hands of a corporal?

The answer came in a sharp tone. "Here, take you papers and go."

With a respectful nod and quick steps up the concrete stairs, he was inside. He checked his overcoat, slipped his identification into his breast pocket, and found a seat on the third row, just as the renowned physicists began his speech. The wooden chair creaked, as he crossed his legs and eased his hand into the pocket that carried his pistol. His fingers fell around the grip like it was made for them. *I'm about to do murder and then poison myself.* And, he breathed a prayer. "Dear God, how did it come to this?"

* * * *

Twenty years before he plotted to kill a man he'd never met, Moe Berg stood gazing out the window at Rue d'Assas and the campus of Sorbonne University. He was nearly as adept with French as he was with his native English, and he said, "I love the sight of Paris in the morning." He walked across the one-room apartment to the kitchenette, where a thin, young woman sat, still dressed in nightwear, eating toast and figs. "Don't you love the morning, Gisselle?"

"Not as much as the nighttime, my sweet. I love the cool of the evening and the mystery of the darkness. In the morning, like today, I must work, and that I do not love." She pushed her plate aside and gestured toward a stack of newspapers piled on the table. "When will you get rid of those papers?"

"Not yet. They're still alive."

"But, some of them are three days old."

"Yes, but they're not dead until I've read them. Still, I suppose I should get them off the table." He gathered the papers into his arms, took heavy steps to the bed, knelt, and pulled two suitcases from beneath it. The lid of the first suitcase clinked against the metal bedrail. He filled it with newspapers, closed the lid, and stood with a suitcase in each hand. "Okay, I guess that's it."

"That's it? What do you mean?"

3

"I mean it's been great, but the winter is nearly over, and I'm due at spring training soon."

Gisselle carried her dishes to the sink, slowly rinsed her hands, and dried them with a small towel. "I don't know what you mean by spring training, but you sound strangely like a man who is about to leave his lover." Moe didn't answer. He didn't need to. He clamored to the door, pausing long enough to kiss her cheek, before setting his suitcases in the hall. She twisted the towel in her hands and said, "Do you have nothing to say to me? After five months together, you leave me without a word of why?"

"Yes, of course, you're entitled to something more than the sight of my back. I'm a baseball player, Gisselle. For Brooklyn. And, in the spring, we go to Florida to get ready for the season. That's spring training. So, clearly, I must get to my ship on time, lest I put my spot on the team in jeopardy. It's just business."

"But, I thought you loved me."

"Hmm, love? I'm not sure I fully appreciate the concept, but I'll give it some thought on the trip home. Oh, by the way, I suppose I should tell you. My name isn't really James. It's Moe." She snatched her plate from the sink, smashed it against the wall, and ran to the bed in tears. Moe studied her for a moment, picked up his suitcases, and muttered, "Well, that didn't go as well as I'd hoped." And, without another word, he left her.

* * * *

With Europe and Gisselle behind him, Moe found a sparkling ocean and sunny skies in Clearwater. He stepped through the gates at the ballpark to be greeted by a ruddy-faced man with a prominent nose and Iowan accent. "Did you walk all the way from the hotel, Moe?"

"Hi, Dazzy. Yes, I like to walk and, to be honest, I never learned to drive."

4

Vance stroked his chin, cast his gaze from Moe's shined shoes to his gray hat, and said, "You're the only guy I ever saw who'd wear a black suit to practice."

"I'm in mourning for the world." Berg stood quietly and then smiled. "Where is Uncle Robbie?"

"In the locker room, trying to figure out who's here and who ain't. There must be fifty guys in camp this year, and probably twenty are pitchers, but I ain't worried."

"Nor should you be, not with your ERA. Well, I suppose I should go let him know I've arrived." Dust puffed with each step, as Moe passed the dugout and navigated his way to the locker room. He found Wilbert Robinson straddling a bench, scribbling notes onto a small pad. "Good morning, coach."

Uncle Robbie answered without looking up. "It's manager, Berg, not coach."

"How did you know it was I without looking?"

Robinson spat tobacco juice to the floor, next to Berg's glossy shoes. "Oh, I had a hint." Then he looked up and drew his left leg across the bench. "Have a seat, Moe. I need to talk to you."

Berg sat with his elbows propped on his knees. "Is there a problem? I know I'm a day late, but my ship had to change course to avoid a storm."

"Then you should've taken an earlier ship, boy, but that's not the problem. The truth is we've decided to option you to Minneapolis."

"You're sending me down?"

"That's right. You had a decent year last season, and you're a good infielder, but you don't hit enough. You know Johnny Mitchell is going to play short, and High will be at second. If we keep you with the team, you'll ride the bench, and that won't help you develop as a player. In the minors, you'll play, and bat, every day. And,

5

the coaches down there will have time to teach you some things."

Moe let out a heavy breath. "Well, I hadn't expected this. My father never wanted me to play ball. Maybe he was right."

"Ah, don't take it so hard. We send guys down all the time. Besides, I looked at your file. My gosh, son, you graduated Magna Cum Laude from Princeton. You speak twelve languages, and they say you have a photographic memory, for goodness sake. You could make a hell of a lot more money in business than you can in baseball. I can't figure out what you're doing here."

"You know how it is, Robbie. I love the game, and so do you."

"Yeah, but don't let the game make a fool of you like it did to me."

"I don't know what you mean."

"You know I was a catcher in my playing days. So, a few years ago, not long before the Great War, we decided to pull a publicity stunt and have a gal drop a ball from a plane for me to catch. Well, she came flying over like she was supposed to, but she forgot to take a ball with her. Why she had a grapefruit on that plane, I don't know, but I think she did it on purpose. That thing busted wide open, spewed sticky stuff all over me. It took me three days to wash that shit off." Moe tried to restrain himself, but a chuckle crept out. "That's better, boy. Sometimes you have to laugh at these things. Now, go to Minnesota and take your medicine like the rest of us."

* * * *

A long, hot summer faded into fall, and Moe Berg went home for Thanksgiving. He sat in the living room, his long legs stretched over a coffee table, reading a book on Greek history. He tried to ignore the sound of his father entering the room and taking the seat across from him, but he couldn't ignore his voice. "So, you are reading again."

"Yes, Papa, I like to read."

"That is good. You can learn a lot of things reading, things that can help you earn a good living."

"I'm making a living. I saved enough to pay my passage to Europe again. I'm going to study in Heidelberg."

"But, this life is not what I wanted for you. You could be a lawyer, a business man, something."

Moe lowered the book into his lap. "Are we going to argue this again?"

"Argue what? I'm only saying that it is good to read."

"I know, but we've had this conversation, and it's always the same. You and Mama didn't move here from the Ukraine and build a life in America, just so I could waste mine with baseball. I'm making a living, Papa. Maybe if you came to see a game, you'd understand why I want to play so badly."

Bernard ran a finger through his thick moustache. "I will not waste my time with sports. They divert the mind from more important things, things like making a living and raising a family. And, look at you, Morris. You are twenty-two years old and you don't have a girlfriend, much less a wife. How will your mother have grandchildren, if you don't marry?"

The answer came from the kitchen door, in soft tones. "I'm not old enough to be a grandmother." Rose circled the sofa and put her hand to the side of Moe's face. "My boy will marry when he's ready, when he finds a good Jewish girl, who will give him lots of fat children."

"I don't know, Mama. Maybe she won't be Jewish."

"You shouldn't tease you mother like that."

"So, you think he is teasing you? Your boy spends his time throwing a baseball around, while his brother is in medical school, and even Ethel is already teaching school. I didn't cross an ocean and . . ."

"Dinner is almost ready. You two men wash your hands. It's time to be thankful for what we have, not to argue over things we cannot change." Bernard started to speak, but she raised a finger. "Not a word more. I won't have it." She ruffled Moe's black hair and said, "Come, I'll pour the wine while you get ready." Then she turned and left with Bernard close behind.

Moe drew his feet from the table, wagged his head, and whispered, "That man will be the end of me." He stood and started toward the bathroom, but stopped when he saw his sister at the dining room table. "What are you doing, Eth?

"Just looking at catalogues and dreaming about a new piano, but I heard you and Daddy."

"He drives me bananas. It's like he wants to control everything I do. I'm a grown man. I've been to Paris."

She turned a crooked grin. "Did you do anything nasty in Paris?"

"What a question for a girl to ask."

She pushed a chair with her foot, scraping it over the wooden floor. "Sit down, little brother. Tell me all about it."

He sat, leaning on one arm. "It was the most beautiful city I've ever seen, especially at night when the lights come on. And, in the daytime, I walked the streets, soaking up the culture, so much art, so much history. I absolutely fell in love with the Louvre."

"Did you fall in love with anything else? You know what I mean."

Moe lowered his voice. "There was this one girl. She had a way about her that was different from anyone I ever knew."

"Did she have some gams?"

"Why, Ethel, I should tweak your nose. Do you think I go about staring at girl's legs? You make me sound like Sam."

"Oh, I hate him. You know why he didn't come for Thanksgiving, don't you?"

"Mama said he was studying for exams of some kind."

"And, what college has exams the week of Thanksgiving? I'll bet he's in the Catskills fooling around with that Hamilton girl. Daddy thinks he's the golden child, the doctor, but he's not so golden when it comes to women. And, he's started smoking too. I smelled it on him."

"Can you keep a secret?"

Her eyes brightened. "Sure."

"That's good to know. Maybe someday I'll have one to tell you."

She punched him in the chest. "You're a bad man, Moe Berg. Not to be trusted."

* * * *

Winter in Germany with another girlfriend, who also thought his name was James, was followed by virtual anonymity in the minor leagues, until September. Moe posted a quick note to his mother and caught the train to Chicago. The White Sox were giving him a chance, and he wanted to make the most of it. He brought three bats, each carefully treated with tobacco spit, but he would need only one that year. Most of his time was spent riding the pine in the dugout reading and writing letters, like the one to his sister.

Hi Ethel,

I hope you are well. Give my love to Mama. Chicago is a lively town with lots of opportunities for a young man to go wrong (insert smile here). The South Side has block parties and carnivals most every night. Don't let on, but I saw a man last evening at a speakeasy that I believe to have been Al Capone. He was a tough looking character, surrounded by body guards. It was thrilling.

I've decided not to spend the winter abroad this year. Yesterday I received the acceptance letter for Columbia University's law school. Maybe that will make Papa happy, at least for now.

Good luck with college. Don't be bad like your brother, and keep in touch.

Moe

Berg toiled away in Chicago, partying at night and earning occasional playing time at third base. His dream of a career in baseball was beginning to fade, perhaps to be replaced with the tedious doldrums of corporate law, until August 1927 in Boston. Once again, he was perched in the dugout, with Manager Ray Schalk on one side and the bulky Buck Crouse on the other. "How's the finger, Buck?" Berg asked.

"No so good. I've been using the salve, like the doc said, but that thing's as sore as a boil." He raised his bandaged middle finger and pointed it at Moe. "Hell, I could outhit you with one hand. With all your learning, you ain't never figured out how to hit the curve ball."

"There's truth in that, Buck. You know, I met a girl in Germany with a finger swollen like yours. She said it made for fun times under the covers. Is that how you use yours?"

Before Crouse could curse, Schalk sprang to his feet. "Oh hell, Carlyle doubled. Did you see that, boys? A damn double." Moe's attention turned from Buck's finger to the field. Two pitches later Pee Wee Wanninger slapped the ball down the first base line. "Look out, he's gonna try to score on that. Block the plate, Harry. Block it?"

Crouse followed Berg to the rail and said, "Shit, man, that was a hell of a collision. It don't look like Harry's getting up." The waited quietly as Schalk sprinted to his fallen catcher, and the crowd cheered Carlyle's strut to his dugout.

The aging manager returned more slowly than he had left. "They're sending for a stretcher. I told him over and over to be careful about blocking the plate." He tossed his cap toward the bench. "Buck, are you up to it?"

"I'd like to, Skipper. I can catch the ball okay, but I can't throw worth a shit."

"Can any of you boys play catcher?"

Silence filled the dugout like a cloud. Then Berg said, "I don't know."

"What's that? You don't know?"

"My high school coach told me I didn't know how to catch."

"Well, hell, son, let's prove him wrong. Get out there."

It had been a long time since Moe Berg had been unsure about anything, but he was now. Maybe this was a chance to stick with the team, and, if he failed, maybe it was a quick way out the door. But, he had to try, if not for the team for himself. He waited until the medical staff carried McCurdy away and then strapped on the gear left strewn behind the plate. As fate would have it, the first pitch was in the dirt, and it skirted past him, sending Wanninger to second. Berg scolded himself. *You can do better than that, Moe. Now concentrate.* A fast ball inside,

11

and the speedy Wanninger took off for third. Berg shifted and fired a strike to the hot corner. Out. Moe's anxiety spilled out of his mouth, as he walked down the baseline, pointing a finger. "You don't steal on Moe Berg, Pee Wee."

Wanninger pulled himself up and said, "Are you talking to me?"

"Yes, I'm talking to you and all those guys on your team. If you get on base, you'd better stay there or I'll bean you before you can get to second." Pee Wee shrugged and trotted across the infield. For three innings, Berg caught an error-less game. In the bottom of the eighth, Wanninger came to bat again with the infamous Carlyle on third. "I apologize for what I said to you, Pee Wee. I was a little excited."

"That's all right, Moe. I'll pay you back by driving my boy in from third."

"You do that. I'll be waiting for him." A sweeping curve ball started inside and cut back to the plate. Wanninger took a big swing and popped it up. Berg sprang from his crouch, tossed his mask aside, and caught the ball. He felt great. Carlyle was stranded, and the catching job might be his. He rolled the ball toward the mound and trotted for the dugout. Then he heard the roar of the crowd. "Damn, there's only two outs."

Carlyle scored and Buck's voice echoed from the rail. "Hell, Moe, you might speak twelve languages, but you can't count to three."

* * * *

The embarrassment of allowing Carlyle to score was softened by the win, and a long train ride. Moe spent the next evening touring the night spots of Chicago. By midnight, he had reached Broadway and the Green Mill Cocktail Lounge with a leggy blonde seated next to him near the bar. "Are you sure you want to stay here?" she asked.

"Why wouldn't we stay?"

"Because Jack McGurn is part owner. They call him Machine Gun McGurn and they say Joe E. Lewis, you know that comedian guy, got his throat cut for not bringing his show here. Jack McGurn is a dangerous man."

"Which is what brings me. I've long been curious about what drives a man to kill, ever since reading about Leopold and Loeb."

"I heard about them on the radio, two rich boys who killed that little girl and stuffed her body in a can, just to see what it feels like. Oh, that's creepy. Come on, sugar, let's blow this pop stand."

"In a minute, but let's have a drink first. Then we'll catch a cab. I promise." She ordered a whiskey sour, and Berg opted for a tall beer. He nursed it for thirty minutes, until the back door opened and four men stepped in, hands in their pockets. Then a stocky man, marked by a scar on his face, passed between them to a table near the short end of the bar. "That's him."

"Who? Oh, my God, don't let him see me."

"I'm going over to talk to him."

"Are you crazy? They'll gun you down."

"Maybe not. Think about it. We're sitting in a bar openly serving alcohol in a time when that is a federal offence, and yet not one police officer has bothered to intervene. They know about this place. Movie stars come here. What's it like to have that kind of influence? He's powerful, but in a quiet way. He hides his crimes in plain view. It's a fascinating study in human behavior."

She rose and clutched her purse to her side. "You do whatever you want, bud. I'm getting out of here."

Moe waved her off, took a final drink of his beer, and stood. Each step toward Capone's table was filled with an exotic mixture of both fear and excitement. He eased by well-dressed men bent over the bar until he was close enough for one of the body guards to hold out his hand. "Excuse me, Mr. Capone. I don't mean to bother you, but I wanted to say hello."

The guard stepped between them and grunted. "Move on while you've got your health."

But, Capone pushed him aside. "Wait a minute. I think I've seen this guy."

"I'm Moe Berg. I play baseball for the White Sox."

"I love baseball. What position do you play?"

"Well, most recently, I've been catching."

"Oh, yeah. You're the guy who let Carlyle score yesterday. Nearly cost us the game." Berg studied him closely, from his dark eyes to the puffy cheeks. "Che cosa stai guardando?" Capone asked.

"Perdonami per essere maleducato."

"So, you speak Italian. That's good. I hear the other players call you the brain,"

"Among other things."

"Well, being smart don't give you the right to stare at me. It ain't healthy."

"That was rude of me, and I apologize, but I find you a most interesting person. You are undoubtedly the most powerful man in the city. On the one hand you support food kitchens, a hero to the downtrodden, and on the other you have clubs that openly operate illegally without interference from the law. It's something of a wonder to see. And I'm curious about how a man, who lives in a world as dangerous as yours, can be so successful."

"My world ain't so different from yours. Tell me, Brain. When a pitcher hits one of your guys with a fast ball, what does your manager do?"

"He has our pitcher hit one of their batters. That's baseball. You let the other team know you won't stand for throwing at your guys."

"And, that's what I do. People in the soup lines never done me no harm, so I help them. But, when somebody horns in on my business, tries to take food from my children, then I bean them and hard, so they don't come calling again." Capone grinned, lit a cigar, and let the smoke trickle from his thick lips. "You want to know how to make it in a tough world? Never let them know what you're thinking, kid. If they don't know, they can't use it against you."

* * * *

Berg avoided the Green Mill for the remainder of his time with the White Sox. He wanted to meet Capone, not get to know him. He fell into the catcher's role like a natural, famous for his strong throwing arm and retiring base runners with little more than a flick of the wrist. And, near the end of the season, he met the man who epitomized baseball in the best and worst ways, Ty Cobb.

The bottom of the sixth inning brought Cobb to the plate. He didn't speak to Berg, opting instead to exchange insults with the pitcher, Sarge Connally. "What part of Texas are you from, boy, the part with all the beaners?"

Connally ignored him, but his manager did not, shouting from the dugout, "You better shut your yap, Cobb, before he puts one in your ear."

"Yeah? Well, how about I knock one over there where you are?"

"I'd like to see you do it." Connally rolled into his windup and delivered a fast ball to the outside of the plate.

Cobb opened his stance and slapped the ball into the dugout, just past Schalk's head. "Damn it, Ty, cut that shit out."

"There's more where that came from, Ray. So, shut the hell up." He pumped his bat three times through the strike zone, like he would blast the next pitch out of the ballpark but, when it came, he dribbled a bunt down the third-base line. The throw to first was not close to getting him, and Cobb howled with laughter. "How'd you like that, Sarge?"

Lu Blue stepped into the batter's box, and Berg trotted out to the mound. "Okay, calm down, Sarge. Don't let Cobb get to you."

"I hate that son of a bitch."

"Yeah, I know he's a loud mouth."

"It's not that, Moe. Lots of guys pop off when they come to bat. What I hate is that Cobb tells you what he's going to do, and then he does it. He rubs your face in it, and I can't seem to get the bastard out."

"Well, he's not at the plate now. Let's get the guy who is." He took his position behind home plate, pulled the mask over his face, and called for a curve ball. Connally shook him off. *Damn, Sarge, you don't want to throw this guy a fastball.* He called the curve again and, again, the pitcher shook his head. So, he put down one finger. Cobb broke for second, as Blue laid down another bunt. Connally scooped the ball up and tossed it to first, but Cobb turned second and raced for third. The throw from first was on time, and Cobb knocked it loose with a high slide. Moe slapped his mitt. "Damn, that guy's fast."

He walked back to the plate, and a shout came from third. "Hey, Jew boy, I'm coming to see you on the next pitch."

Don't do it, Moe. Don't let him bait you.

"Do you hear me down there? You're gonna think hell broke loose when I get there, boy. Why don't you step aside and just let me stroll in, so nobody gets hurt? If you don't, I'll have to send you home to your mama early today."

Well, shit. You had to mention my mother, didn't you? Moe called for a timeout, laid his mask and mitt on the plate, and took deliberate steps down the baseline. When he reached third, he offered his hand. "It's an honor for me to shake hands with the greatest player ever to strap on baseball spikes, Mr. Cobb."

"Well, thank you, son. You're smarter than I thought."

"I do want to share a thought with you, though. Please look at me. I am six-feet-three-inches tall, and I weigh well over two-hundred pounds. You are welcome to charge toward home plate as hard as you like but, if you come in with your spikes high, I will put my best effort into breaking your leg."

"Is that right?"

"Hell yes, it's right. Now, you have a good rest of the game. It's been a pleasure."

The next batter sailed a long, fly ball to right field, and Cobb easily trotted home. He winked at Berg as he touched the plate and said, "Well, I reckon we didn't have to find out who the better man is today, but maybe another time."

"I'll be here, Mr. Cobb, right here."

Chapter Two

Moe filled his summers with baseball, and spent the winters in law school, anxiously awaiting the arrival of March and spring training. He had privately known many women, but his one real romance was with the sport his father didn't want him to play, and she was about to toy with his affections. The sixth day of April brought the White Sox to Arkansas to play an exhibition game with the Little Rock Travelers. Moe was barely twenty-eight years old, but the long bus ride left his back sore and his temper short. After four innings of stooping behind home plate, his back began to loosen, but his patience grew thinner and thinner with each epithet thrown by the opposing catcher when he came to bat in the top of the innings. He knocked dirt from his spikes and stepped into the batter's box, and the catcher started again. "Hey, Berg, you're a Jew bastard, a kike."

Moe stepped out and adjusted his cap. "I'm disappointed in you, Louie. You called me those identical names during my first at bat. Have you no imagination. Perhaps I can help with a few alternatives. Try words like Abraham, heeb, shieeny, or Christ killer; although, I must say I hold Christ in the highest regard. But, feel free to use any of those choices. There is no fee."

"You shit ass."

"That I won't deny, you thick-headed dago, guinea, wop, but don't come out of your crouch, or your fans will see me beat you like the dumbass you are." Berg eased back into the box, ensuring his practice swing was low enough to brush the catcher's head. Then he turned his gaze to the mound and right-hander Byron Humphrey, the baggy legs of his trousers fluttering in a mild breeze. *So, let's see. Last time you started me with two fast balls and*

18

then a curve. I'll wager the curve comes first this time. Come on, Slick, let me see it. Humphrey rocked into a pump-handle windup and delivered the pitch side-armed. A red dot appeared in the center of the ball, and Moe kept his hands back until it broke toward the plate. He cracked a hard grounder just out of the reach of the shortstop and plodded his way to first base.

He felt great, not just to have a base hit, but now he was beginning to understand the psychology of pitching. This could be the beginning of something. He took his lead off first, still grinning, and Humphrey turned with a quick pickoff throw. Moe dove back toward first, but his spikes caught the dirt and something went terribly wrong. He tumbled down with pain shooting across his knee and up his thigh. "No, no, no! Not now."

* * * *

Moe had always been comfortable at institutes of learning. He insisted that his mother let him follow Sam and Ethel to school when he was but three years old. The University of Arkansas was inviting, but not as inviting in the medical center. He sat on the edge of a gurney with his right knee heavily wrapped and bound with a splint. Well, doctor, what's the verdict?" he asked.

"It isn't good, Mr. Berg. You've sheared a ligament in that knee."

"Okay, can you fix it? How soon can I play ball again?"

"Fix it? That's an interesting question. If you were a shopkeeper or maybe a banker, I'd try to do exactly that, and then I'd send you back to work with a cane. But, you are neither of those. You're an athlete and, not only an athlete, but a major-league ball player. If you are to return to your profession, you're going to need the level of care I'm just not qualified to provide you."

"I'm not following you, Doc. Are you referring me to another physician?"

Ray Schalk stepped around the gurney and said, "Why don't you let me talk to him?" And, the doctor walked away. "Look, Moe, these guys just ain't got what it takes to work on a professional athlete. There's a train that leaves here at eight o'clock headed to St. Louis, and then another one to Chicago. We're going to get you to Mercy Hospital. "

"I appreciate that, Skipper. They have an excellent facility."

"Well, it's the least we can do. I can't promise you that Mr. Comiskey will pay for it. You know what a tightwad he is, but I'll try." He hesitated and then said, "I've got to be honest with you, boy. If that knee don't heal up soon, he'll let you go."

"I am well aware of that, Ray, but it's going to heal. It has to." Moe lay back and asked to be let alone. Surrounded by the scent of alcohol and the faint cries of other patients down the hall, his solitude comforted him in a way no one could. A silent scream cut through his soul, and he swore that nothing would stop him. "Nothing, damn it. Nothing."

* * * *

Moe left the hospital on crutches and, in two weeks, advanced to a cane. But, his recovery was still much slower than he could stand. Nights were short, his sleep interrupted by shooting pains in the knee. Ice packs every morning and afternoon kept swelling at bay, but only if he stayed off his feet. He stood in the kitchen, bracing himself against the table, and trying to ease into the catcher's squat. Something popped, and with an "Oh shit" he collapsed onto the tile floor. "Damn it, damn it, damn it." He rolled over, the cold tile against his back and lay twenty minutes, thinking about a future without baseball. Future? Pretending to be a lawyer was more like bondage than a career. Then he pulled himself up and tried again. The best he could manage was kneeling on one knee with the other stretched out flat, and he knew that just wouldn't make it in the majors.

When the end of April kissed the first of May, he found himself riding with Ray Schalk to the upper corner of Wisconsin. "You know, I wouldn't have to drive all the way from Chicago to Eagle River, if you'd learn to drive, Moe."

"You're right about that, but I'm not convinced this knee would let me work a clutch just yet."

"Well, if you want to keep your job with the team, you won't tell Mr. Comiskey that. He don't want to hear what a player's going to look like in the spring. I tried to tell him you're doing real good, but if he don't think you can help us this year, he'll bring in another catcher, and there ain't a thing I can do about it. He'll do the same with me, if we don't start winning more games."

"I understand, Ray, and I appreciate your bringing me. And, I appreciate your hedging on the extent of my knee injury. If I can get by this year, I should be okay for spring training." He turned his gaze from Schalk to the windshield. "Wow, is that his place?"

"That's it. Now, you see where all that money goes."

"It is impressive, as big as a church and a spectacular view of the water." The Chrysler rocked to a stop near the porch, and Berg tossed his cane into the back seat. "Very well, then, let's see what the old man has to say." He shoved the heavy, steel door open and stood to a sharp pain that shot from his knee into his thigh. Six miserable steps brought him the porch and five more to the door. Schalk started to ring the doorbell, but Moe stopped him.

"Hang on a second." He wiped perspiration from his brow and tucked his handkerchief back into his coat pocket. "All right, Ray. Go ahead."

A tall, black man appeared at the door and escorted them through the house, out the back door, and to a cabana next to the pool. Comiskey sat with a cigar in one hand and a glass of scotch in the other. His double chin waggled as he spoke. ""Hello Ray, Moe. I asked you to come here, because I don't do much business at the office anymore. Heart problems, you know, and my doctor has confined me to this elegant prison. Have a seat, and let's talk business."

Moe's leg burned as he sat, and his stomach turned sour from the pain, but he fought them both. "Good afternoon, Mr. Comiskey. Thank you for inviting us to your home."

"Yeah, well, I'd offer you a cocktail, but I don't expect we'll be here long enough for you to drink it, so here's the thing. We brought you to the White Sox because we thought you could help us, certainly not with your bat, but you're a fine catcher and, to be honest, you have some other qualities as well that can be good for business."

"I'm not following you, sir. "

"Sir? You weren't calling me that a few months ago, when you wanted more money. What was it? Oh yes, the Old Roman, skinflint, cheapskate. I believe those were your terms then."

"They were, and those words are hard to swallow, but I didn't come here to beg. When you say 'other qualities', if you're talking about a job in the front office, I appreciate that, but I want to play ball."

"Front office? Hell, I don't need you there. You're a smart guy, even made the papers, sports writers telling the whole country about the Professor. When my people told me about that, I thought the notoriety might sell a few tickets. Then they told me you're a Jew. We've been trying to increase our appeal to the Jewish community for some time, but there are other Jew players without bum knees."

"But, my knee is healing very quickly. As you can see, I walked in with no trouble at all."

Comiskey took a draw on his cigar, looked at Schalk, and said, "Is that right, Ray? Is this boy's knee well?"

"Well, I, uh, I can't say it's completely well, but he's coming along real good. Once we get him back on the field, we'll see how he does behind the plate. That'll tell everything we need to know."

"I don't believe you. In fact, I had the team physician look at the reports from the hospital. He tells me this young man is at least a year away from serious competition, and he probably will never play at the major-league level again." A long, quiet moment passed. "Look at me, Moe. I like to look at a man when I tell him he's fired."

"I am looking at you, and I rode nearly seven hours, so you could have the pleasure of firing me in person. I would think a man in your condition would savor the days he has left and not waste them on trivial matters like firing a second-string catcher."

Comiskey seemed to ignore him, but he smiled. "Ray, take Mr. Berg back to Chicago and, when you get there, put him on waivers. If he can convince some other team that he's well, maybe we can pick up something in return."

"Yes, sir. Come on, Moe. I think we should go now."

"Another team? Damn right." He stumbled through the house and stopped at the front door. "Ray, would you get my cane for me? I don't think I can make it to the car."

23

* * * *

Dear Ethel,

I had great hopes when Cleveland picked up my contract but, alas, they have now released me. My heart·is heavy, but Papa should be happy, since I am now forced to play lawyer on Wall Street with Satterlee and Canfield. I do find it fascinating that the very rich still have money to invest in the midst of this depression, while many are forced to eat the apples they hoped to sell on the streets or stand in line at the soup kitchens. But then, I'm a bit cynical just now. I am hopeful that walking the streets of New York will strengthen my knee, though I fear just the opposite. When you get a day off, come and see me. I could use some cheering up.

Love to all,

Moe

P.S. Keep this quiet, but I heard that Herb Hunter is planning another trip to Japan to teach them about baseball. Hoping to tag along.

* * * *

His gray fedora hung on the back of his office door, just above the black suit coat, while Moe sat in his chair winding a rubber band through his fingers. He wondered whether he should shine his shoes. He'd shined them two days before, but perhaps the street dust could be buffed away. *What's that noise? It sounds like, no, it can't be.* The thin frame of Ethel Berg rolled to a stop at his open door, atop a pair of roller skates with another pair dangling by its strings from her shoulder. He rose to his feet, his heart brimming. "Ethel, what brings you to town?"

"You said for me to come and see you, didn't you?"

"Yes, but I thought I'd meet you at the station."

"Well, I'm here now and ready for some lunch."

"That's fine. Let me get my jacket. I know a great Italian place on Seventh." She pulled the pair of skates from her shoulder and held them out. "And, exactly what is that?"

"I brought them for you, so you don't have to pound the concrete every day. Skating will help your knee without putting too much stress on it."

He took the skates and let the string hang over his palm. Then he sat down and asked, "Did you bring a key? Uh, I take that back. You always have a skate key." He clamped a skate to each shoe and gingerly stood. "Let's go." Slowly down the hall and to the lobby. He spoke to the receptionist, as they sailed past. "Going to lunch with my sister, Irene."

"Okay, Mister, uh . . ."

The doorman nodded as they breezed onto the sidewalk. "You know, I think you may be right about this, Eth."

"Of course, I'm right. If you'd come to me instead of those trainers, you'd have finished the season with the Indians. Oh, that reminds me. What's the deal on Japan?"

They dropped off the curb into the crosswalk with horns blaring. "I think I'm in. Herb is taking Lou Gehrig, Ted Lyons, and Left O'Doul so far, and there may be a few more by the time we leave. It'll give me a chance to practice my Japanese and see what the other side of the world looks like."

"How long will you be gone?"

"Oh, a couple of months, but I think I'll stay a bit longer, maybe visit China, even Russia, if the money doesn't run out."

"What does your law firm think about your leaving for so long?"

"Whatever they think I can't let that keep me from going where I want to go, when I want to go."

She laughed. "You are the free spirit, brother. I must admit that."

"Maybe so. By the way, I talked to my friend Walter Johnson, the Big Train, and he made a few calls. If my knee heals well enough, the Senators are willing to take a look at me for next year's roster."

"Baseball put you on a cane, Moe. Are you sure you want to risk it again?"

"I have to try, Eth. Baseball is my lover, even if she hurts me, and I just won't work at something I don't love. I can't."

She swung behind him to avoid a woman carrying a bag of groceries. "Is that why you've never had a serious girlfriend, Moe?"

"Come up here. I don't like talking to people behind me." He waited till she rolled up beside him. "That's better. Here, let's turn into Riverside Park."

"Good choice. This is nice, but you didn't answer my question."

"Technically, I just haven't answered it yet." He turned to his sister and grinned. "All right, the truth is that I've known lots of women, but I'm not interested in anything serious."

"I'm sure you've known plenty of girls, in the Biblical sense, but one-nighters don't make for a happy Moe. You should get out more, meet some people."

They coasted to a stop, and he turned to her. "Look who's talking, Ethel. You're two years older than I am, and I don't see you out looking for a man. What happened to the last one, that Peterson guy?"

"He wasn't the most recent. I've been seeing an English teacher at my school, but I broke if off last week. I want to find the right man, the one meant for me, the guy who makes my heart fly, and he was none of those things. So, I dumped him."

"And, you think I should be on the lookout for the girl meant for me? Not likely, Sis. I fear that woman does not exist. I'm a man destined to die alone, but I'm going to have a good time until I do."

"Don't say that, Moe. You don't mean it, not really. But, one day you may have to make the choice between this carefree lifestyle of yours and the woman who makes you happy."

He scratched the side of his nose and said, "You may be right, but in the meantime I think I'll skate with my sister and play baseball as long as I can. Besides, to be honest, no woman in her right mind would saddle herself with a guy like me."

"Maybe that's what you need, Morris, a woman who is a little out of her mind."

* * * *

While Lake Placid readied itself for the 1932 Olympics, Moe Berg sailed to Japan with Ted Lyons and Lefty O'Doul. He spent two-and-a-half weeks at sea, with a brief stopover in Hawaii, and finally docked at Yokohama Harbor. The trio of American players visited three of the six universities, teaching their players the intricacies of hitting and fielding, and they reached Tokyo Imperial University in late October. They toured the campus, passed through the Red Gate, but stopped when they reached the auditorium. Berg turned to their guide. "Akito, much of what we've seen reflects traditional Japanese design, but this building is brick, and it has a clock tower. Is there an American influence here?"

"Perhaps there could be a Western influence, but our people would never say American, certainly not in our present situation with the United States."

"Yes, I understand the conflict over your incursions in China, but my question is of historical interest, not political."

"I'm afraid everything is political for us, when it comes to America. As much as we appreciate your visit, I must confess that we offered the invitation with trepidation. We have no guarantee of continued funding for our operations, if we offend the imperial government."

"And, I suppose that's why you spread our training sessions over six campuses instead of bringing all your athletes here."

"As your people say, 'There is safety in numbers.' But, I hope you won't let politics keep you from enjoying the beauties of Tokyo. In fact, I have arranged for us to have dinner at a private club tonight."

Berg slapped O'Doul on the shoulder and said, "There you go, Lefty. You won't starve after all."

O'Doul lowered his gaze. "Hell, Moe, I didn't say I was going to starve. I just don't want to eat worms and raw fish, that kind of stuff."

Akito smiled and said, "I am here to meet all your needs. What would you like for dinner, Mr. O'Doul?"

"Call me Lefty, everybody does. And, if I had my druthers, it'd be T-bone steak, medium rare and a cold beer."

"Then you shall have it. Shall I have your geishas call for you at seven?"

"Geishas? What's that?"

"What he's telling you, Lefty, is that we'll be escorted to dinner by ladies, young women trained in the arts, cuisine, and conversation. But, don't assume more than that. They're not prostitutes."

"I wasn't saying that, and you know it. Besides, I ain't the one who shacked up with the hotel doctor's wife."

"Now, Lefty, that was just a nasty rumor, one I've tried to put to rest, if guys like you would let me. Having said that, in my view, the good doctor did an excellent job in selecting his mate." He turned a sly grin and said, "Seven o'clock will be perfect."

* * * *

A heavy fragrance wafted through the gentlemen's club, as Moe Berg sat next to Lefty O'Doul, each of them sandwiched between two geishas. He sniffed the air, looked across the table, and asked, "What is that, Akito? It smells heavy and yet delicate."

"It is agarwood. Some customers find it helps them relax and enjoy their evening."

O'Doul snarled. "It don't make me relax, but another drink might."

"I think we've both had enough to drink, Lefty. We don't want to impose on the hospitality of our host."

"Impose? Hell, all I want to impose on is this little gal sitting beside me."

"That I must ask you not to do." Akito answered. "These young women are specially trained to entertain their guests, but their service has its limits. I can offer you an alternative, if you wish." The two Americans turned a curious look, and he said, "Come, I will show you." They crossed the club floor and passed through heavy, red curtains to another room. Both side walls were lined with upright cabinets with glass fronts and nude dancers in each. "This room is reserved for special guests. The dancers are there for you."

O'Doul cocked his head to one side. "I don't get it. How're we going to get down to business when they're closed up like that?"

"You misunderstand, Lefty. I read about this on the ship. There are holes cut into the glass doors. What Akito is telling you is that you can look and you can touch, but that's as far as it goes. Here, let me demonstrate." Berg stepped to one of the cases, warmed his hands in his arm pits, and then slipped them through the openings in the glass. The girl continued to dance, as he stroked her hips. His hands were on her body, but his gaze was on her eyes, and her expression never changed. No matter how intimate his touches, she remained stoic. He pulled his hands out and stepped back.

"Is something wrong?" Akito asked. "Does she not please you?"

"No, she's lovely. I'm afraid I don't please myself. If you'll excuse me, I need to take a walk." He didn't wait for an answer, but hurried out of the club and onto the sidewalk. His breath misted in the cool air, as he took long strides. Where was he going? He didn't know, but he wasn't happy with where he'd been. Had his life become so hollow that the touch of a woman's body left him empty? Maybe his father was right, and every breath he took was wasted. He spent the night pacing the streets and trying to understand who he was becoming.

* * * *

When his teammates returned to America, Moe was not with them. He wandered from Japan to China and on to Saigon. In Cambodia he slept in an elevated bed to escape snakes in the night. He walked the Great Wall, stood on a pyramid in Egypt, and finally landed in the British Mandate of Palestine. A lonely ride in a Jeep brought him to the summit of a hill overlooking the Valley of Jehoshaphat, a Jew standing on the land that once belonged to his ancestors, but no more. Time slowed, as he waited for something, not quite sure what it might be. Then he felt a stirring in his soul, like the spirits of lives long past filtered through him. And, he muttered the ancient words of the prophet Joel. "Let the nations be roused; let them advance into the Valley of Jehoshaphat, for there I will sit to judge all the nations on every side." He drew in a breath of hot, dry air and tossed a rock down the embankment. "I've nearly circled the earth, only to find myself in a place of judgment, and I don't even know who I am."

Chapter Three

Spring training in Biloxi won Moe a backup spot with the Washington Senators, but only until July, when they released him. It was more of the same. He called a great game, had a terrific throwing arm, but he didn't hit enough. In early August he sat alone in the dining room of the Wardman Park Hotel, sipping a glass of white burgundy, a stack of newspapers resting on the chair beside him. And, he noticed a tall, young woman standing near the entrance. Their gazes met, and she smiled. *Who is that, and why is she smiling at me?*

Her straight skirt hugged narrow hips, as she approached his table and offered her hand. "I'm sorry to be late, but I had trouble finding a cab."

"Yes, of course you did." He pulled out a chair, waited for her to sit, and then returned to his seat. "Taxis can be such a bother this time of day."

"Well, shall we get down to business?"

"Uh, sure, if you like. Can I offer you some wine?"

"You do realize that we're still under the prohibition laws, don't you?"

"I do. Would you like some wine?"

"Yes, thank you." He waved to the waiter for another glass, poured a respectful serving, and watched her embrace the bouquet before taking her first drink. "Is that Pouilly-Fuisse?"

"Oh, a lady after my own heart, who can identify my favorite wine by its taste and texture."

"I recognize it, but I'd prefer Chablis. Ah, enough of that. I assume you have the papers?"

"Indeed I do. I have the *Post*, the *Times*, the *Herald*, and the *Sentinel*."

"No, no, Mr. Paddigan. I'm asking about the contracts, the legal papers."

He rolled the stem of his wine glass between his fingers and said, "I suppose it's time that I confess that, while I am a lawyer, I am not your Mr. Paddigan and I have no contracts. My name is Moe Berg."

"Berg? Why you charlatan. How dare you deceive me like this?"

"You sat at my table. I didn't sit at yours, and please call me Moe."

"Yes, but you should've told me." She looked across the room and then back to Moe. "I'm afraid I've missed my appointment."

He held up her glass. "Waiter, bring us a fresh glass and a bottle of Chablis."

She leaned back and folded her arms. "That's rather bold of you, Mr. Berg, to assume that I would stay after your little charade." She sat quietly until the new glass and bottle arrived and then said, "You haven't even asked my name."

"I thought I'd get you drunk first."

"What a cad you are, a crude and oafish lout."

"I am all those things. Here, drink your wine. Now, what's your name?"

"Estella Huni, and I came here to meet a real estate lawyer about selling some property."

"May I call you Stella?"

"No one calls me that, not even my family."

"Then I shall be the first. Huni is an unusual name, but I've heard it. Let's see, yes, a music school of some kind."

"You are not quite the oil can I thought you might be, Moe Berg. My father owned the New Haven School of Music. When he died, it passed to me, and now I'd like to sell it and move to New York. Now, I have told you my business, and it's only fair that you tell me yours."

"Oh, nothing as exciting as selling a music school. I'm meeting a friend, Walter Johnson." She said nothing. "Walter Johnson, the Big Train."

"Is your friend an engineer?"

"You've never heard of Walter 'Big Train' Johnson? He was one of the greatest pitchers to ever play baseball. He had a fastball that made batters wither at the plate."

"Perhaps I have heard of him. I am not unlearned in sports, but why would the greatest pitcher in history lunch with a man who takes advantage of ladies?"

"He's managing the Indians now, and he wants me to catch for them."

"Then what will he do with Glenn Myatt?"

Myatt broke his, wait a minute. Are you hustling me?"

"Naturally. I thought it only fair, since you led me on the way you did. Of course, I know who Walter Johnson is. Who doesn't? And, I've heard of Moe Berg on the radio, the Professor, if that's who you really are."

"That is who I am; although, just now I'm not so sure." A broad grin crawled over his face. "Have dinner with me tonight, Stella."

Her face softened. "I can't. My train leaves in an hour. I have barely enough time to make it."

He reached for her hand. "Then take a later train. I'll make you glad you did.

"I'll bet you would." She stood, slowly pulled her hand away, and walked toward the door. Then she stopped and turned. "When you get to the city, look me up."

"I'm travelling back to Japan when the season is over. It may be a while before I get to New York."

"If you truly want to see me, you'll find a way."

* * * *

34

Cleveland played the Yankees on August 22nd. Moe didn't see Estella, but he called her from the train station. "Stella?"

"This is Estella Huni, oh, is that you?"

"In the flesh."

"Yes, yes, now what was your name again? Marty?"

"Okay, I should've called sooner, but I'm in New York, at Grand Central, and I've only got thirty minutes before we leave for Boton. I wanted to show up at your building and surprise you, but I don't have the time."

"Yes, time can be fickle. We seem to spend it on the things we think are important. I understand. We met only the one time, you're a bigtime baseball player, and, well, you've only been in town three days to play the Yankees. I read the papers, Moe."

"Wow, you like to pitch inside, don't you? Look, can we get past all that? I'd like to see you. The team will be headed back to Cleveland after this series. The game should be over by four-thirty, and I can be here by eight. Have dinner with me. I know a nice place."

She hesitated and then said, "I'll think about it. You can call me when you get back to town, and we'll see."

"Don't be like that. We'll have a swell time, and I'll be good. I promise."

"Slow down, Moe. Call me at the end of the season, okay?"

"I guess it'll have to be. Just don't change your phone number in the meantime, or I'll have to hunt you down."

There was something in her voice that drew him in, something in her absence that made him hungry to see her. But, even an expensive dinner couldn't take away his commitments. When the season ended, he boarded the

Empress of Japan for another long voyage to the other side of the world. This time it felt even father.

* * * *

The ocean breeze ruffled his wavy hair, as Moe stood by the rail, waiting for his ship to disembark, but it was late. A short, neatly dressed man, carrying a leather case neared. "Pardon me, are you Moe Berg?'

"I am, sir, and to whom do I have the pleasure?"

"My name is Treadwell, and I am with MovietoneNews. I'm sure you've seen our features at the theaters."

"Sure, between the cartoon and the movie. News of the world, isn't it?"

"News of the world and much more. We also bring our viewers footage from exotic places, the kinds of places they'll never visit, but we take them there by way of film. And, that is why I'm here. In this case I have an eight millimeter camera and twenty-four rolls of film. I'm authorized to offer you a contract for movies you shoot, while on your trip to Tokyo."

"How much are we talking about?"

"That's negotiable, but I assure you we'll be fair. Of course, we'd like to see the quality of the film before we buy it."

Moe turned with his back against the rail. "What kinds of things would you like to see?"

"You know, tourist attractions, the Imperial Palace, . shots of the other players in Japan."

"So, you'd like me to film Babe Ruth and Lou Gehrig eating sushi and drinking rice wine?"

"Yes, the players and, you know, the city."

"Hmm, the city. How about footage of the harbor, industrial complexes, military installations?" Moe didn't expect an answer. "Let's not pussyfoot on this. This ship didn't delay its departure so MovietoneNews could offer me a few bucks for tourist movies. Hitler has been trying to align himself with other nations, Argentina, Brazil, and, yes, Japan. You want to know whether they're building an arsenal for war."

"These are troubled times. We tried to limit the size of the Japanese navy, but they ignored us, and now Japan has withdrawn from the League of Nations. They look like a nation that is picking for a fight, and we've got nobody on site to tell us what's going on." Treadwell handed Moe the case. "Do you love your country, Mr. Berg?"

"Love my country? You dare ask whether I love me country? I feel as Montaigne did about Paris. 'I love her so tenderly that even her spots, her blemishes, are dear to me.' I haven't loved many things in my life, but I do love America."

"Then, help her."

* * * *

A dark complexion stretched over six-feet-two inches and two-hundred-sixty pounds of Babe Ruth. His face showed the signs of too many days under the hot sun of summer and too many nights spent with little sleep. But, that didn't keep him from wearing swimming trunks and a sleeveless undershirt, while sitting poolside on the ship with a tall beer in one hand and a cigar in the other. He gestured toward the diving board and said, "Hey, Moe, watch this." He tossed a silver dollar into the water and watched a slender, young woman dive in to retrieve it. "Look at that, boy. She's a limber as a noodle. Her name's Peggy."

"I know. We played chess yesterday. Bright girl. You do realize she's the niece of the Canadian prime minister, don't you?"

"Who gives a damn about Canada? All they've got going for them is good liquor, and you can't hardly get that anymore without paying through your nose for it."

"That could have something to do with Prohibition, Babe. The cost of doing business goes up when half your shipments are impounded at the border. But, I don't believe whiskey is the vice you have in mind just now."

"Well, if we're going to be stuck on this boat for two weeks, I might have to take a run at that."

"What about your wife?"

"Claire? She knows I like to play around. She don't care."

"What if you found Claire, as you say, playing around?"

"Hell, I'd kill her. Any man's got the right to kill a woman who cheats on him, her and the guy she's with. And, don't get no ideas, Moe. I've heard about how you get around."

"That may be true, but young girls like that one are trouble. I'll make you a deal. You keep your paws off her and, when we get to Tokyo, I'll take you to a club where you can feel up all the girls you want."

"Really? They've got those kinds of places there? They say the Japanese girls do it standing up. Is that right?" He threw another coin into the pool, but this time he didn't watch the girl. "Well, is it?"

"I can't say whether that is true or not, but I met a woman in Cambodia who had sex standing on one foot with the other leg sticking straight up in the air. The line of men waiting grew so long, they had to draw lots for a chance to be with her."

"You're bullshitting me."

"She was keeping so many men away from their jobs that it started affecting the local economy, and the government stepped in, and then all the wives came out in force."

"Did they run her off?"

"To the contrary. The wives wanted her to stay. They said they could use the rest."

"Shit, Moe, you're the damnedest liar I ever met."

"Well, I'm working on it, hoping to hone a skill that might come in handy one day."

"Well, if it does, you'll be good at it. Say, what happened to Gehrig?"

"Oh, Lou is in his cabin. He seems to have come down with a case of intestinal fortitude."

"Is it serious?"

"No, he should be ready to play when we get to Japan."

"I'm glad to hear that. Lou had a good year at the plate." He paused and took a puff from his cigar. "He had a hell of a lot better year than I did."

"You did all right, Babe. What did you hit, in the two-eighties?"

"Yeah, but that's a long way from my usual batting average. I'm going downhill, Moe, and the Yankees know it. Look at me. I've gained forty-five pounds since I came to New York. I got away with being the fat guy on the team when I was hitting, but now I think they're done with me."

"The end comes for all of us in time. Have you thought about what you'll do?"

"I tried to get the manager's job with the Yankees, but Mr. Ruppert won't give it to me. I've heard talk that he's trying to trade me to the Braves, and I'd be okay with that, if I can play and manage. Hell, I like Boston." He took another puff and a swig of beer. "What about you? I guess you'll just move over to being a Manhattan lawyer and make your fortune on Wall Street."

"More fortunes seem to have been lost on Wall Street than made lately. Frankly, I'm not sure what I'll do. Not many teams offer manager's jobs to second-string catchers. "

"Then be one of those announcers on the radio. You could call each inning in a different language."

"Radio? It is the hot thing all right, and I don't picture it ever going away, but not as an announcer. I got a letter from a guy about appearing on a program called *Information Please*. Do you know it?"

"Claire listens to it. People write in with questions, right?"

"Yes, they have a panel of experts who are challenged with answering questions on topics ranging from the sciences to modern art to bowling. They seem to think a college-educated, Jew, lawyer, ball player might win more listeners. The program is broadcast from New York, and I have reasons to be in New York when we get back."

"What kind of reasons, you dog?"

"Personal reasons, Bambino, personal reasons."

* * * *

Berg's escort from two years ago brought two open-topped cars to pick the players up when they reached the dock. Moe, Ruth, and Gehrig rode in the first car, with Akito sitting up front, while Jimmie Foxx, Earl Averill, Lefty Gomez, and Connie Mack followed in the second car. They represented a snap shot of American all-stars, and then there was Moe Berg the backup catcher. He wasn't sure why he'd been invited again. Maybe it was to demonstrate his skill in calling games or his ability to throw out runners or maybe they just needed a guy who could speak Japanese. Whatever the reason, he was glad to be there and quietly astir with the prospect of filming sensitive part of the city without anyone knowing why.

"Hey, Lou, are you feeling all right now?" Ruth asked.

"Sure, I'm as fit as a fiddle. Why do you ask?"

"Moe said you were down with a case of intestinal fortitude. I think I had that once when I tried some Chinese food. Man, I was on the john for a week."

"Babe, intestinal fortitude is . . ."

Berg interrupted. "Akito, Tokyo is a big city, but most of the buildings I see are only a story or two high. Why are there no skyscrapers?"

"Some have suggested that we should, indeed, build taller buildings to better house the population, but our laws limit our ability to do that. No building can be tall enough to look down on the Imperial Palace."

"What about the one out there in the distance?"

"That is Saint Luke's Hospital, and it is far enough away so that, even if one stood on top of it, he would not look down on the palace."

"Good, I suppose we now know where to go in case any of our intestinal problems should come back to visit."

"I trust you will not need to visit the hospital and I suggest that you not wander outside the hotel without my being with you. Suspicions are running quite high between our people and the United States. All Americans, even athletes, are considered to be spies until proven otherwise."

"Are you trying to frighten us, Akito?"

"Perhaps. A frightened man is a careful man. The world is becoming a dangerous place, and you must be careful in my city."

* * * *

Dear Stella,

I hope this cablegram finds you well. Tokyo is as beautiful as I remembered it, and I wish you could be here

41

to share it with me. We've played three games so far and have throttled the local players in each. Japanese pitching is like taking batting practice for these mugs. The crowd shouts "Banzai Ruth" every time Babe comes to the plate, and I've never seen Foxx in better condition. We're having a grand time, but I miss you. We have but a few games left, and then the team will split up. Babe is going back through London. He wants to see a game of cricket, and I hope to see Moscow before returning home. Perhaps you could meet me there. Think about it.

  Moe

None of the players asked why Berg chose to skip the game in Omiya. He was often known to disappear after ball games or to leave a dinner table and not return. And, no one knew his idiosyncrasies better than Moe himself, and he was expert in using them to excuse himself when he had better things to do. He stood before his hotel room mirror with his hair parted down the middle, his bare feet squeezed into a pair of geta, and a black kimono wrapped around his broad body. "You're a bit tall to pass yourself off as Japanese, but let's give it a try." He pulled flowers from the vase on the dresser, wrapped their stems with one of his newspapers, and called the front desk for a taxi.

He drew a few stares as he passed through the lobby and, when he reached the sidewalk, he found a rickshaw waiting. "Not exactly what I had in mind, but one makes do." The slow ride to Saint Luke's gave him time to see the parts of the city hidden to tourists. Children played juggling games, while the streets teemed with adult faces drawn into frowns. There was nothing beautiful in the alleys, nothing that made him want to visit them again. When he reached the hospital, he attracted more stares. Would his Japanese be good enough to allow for his odd

42

appearance? The receptionist didn't challenge him, until he asked for Elsie Lyon's room number. "She is the daughter of the American ambassador. Why do you come to see her?"

"I am but a servant delivering flowers."

"Who has sent you to deliver these flowers?"

"The baseball players who are traveling here. I work at the hotel where they are staying."

Her face seemed to doubt him, but she said the words he wanted to hear. "Room 517."

He found the elevator and stood watching the dial over the doors, until the car arrived. He stepped in, closed the doors, and shifted the handle to UP. The most direct route was to go straight to the top floor, but it occurred to him that someone might watch the same dial he watched to see where he got off. So, he stopped at the fifth floor, got off, dumped his flowers into a trash can, and boarded again. The short ride to the seventh floor was thrilling. He was afraid, but excited as well. The hallway was nearly empty, but he didn't hurry. He exited through a heavy door at the end of the hall onto the roof. The view covered half the city, but there was a better spot. His hard sandals clattered on metal steps, as he wound his way up a spiral staircase to the bell tower.

When he reached the top, he pulled the camera from his kimono and panned the landscape, moving counterclockwise from one opening to another. His hand trembled. *Come on, settle down. A bad movie is as bad as no movie.* Then a calm swept over him, as the shipyards came into view. This is why he came, to shoot ships and factories and anything the Japanese could use to make war. Then he heard the metallic click of the roof door opening again. He pulled the camera close to his chest and leaned against the wall. *Oh crap, I'm caught. They'll throw me in prison as a spy, if not worse.*

An armed guard stepped to the bottom of the bell tower, and then he came in, but he didn't come up the stairs. Maybe he could surprise the guard, knock him down, and run. *Yeah, run in sandals. That's a laugh. And, how do I sneak down a spiral, steel staircase? You've done it now, Moe.* Then a waft of smoke reached his nostrils, and he grinned. *The guy snuck in here to have a cigarette. I should turn him in.*

In the time it took the guard to finish his smoke and return to the building, Moe was on his way down the staircase. He stuffed the camera back into his kimono, rode the elevator down, and hurried out of the building without a word. The rickshaw was almost half way back to the hotel before his heart stopped pounding. "I did it," he whispered. "Perhaps not my best effort, but, damn it, not bad. I think I might be a spy."

* * * *

The following day found Berg in uniform, ready to play the Tokyo Giants. As he walked toward the bullpen, he heard Connie Mack's voice call from behind. "Hey, Moe, hold up."

"Oh, hi Mr. Mack. Do you need something?"

"You're going to be in the lineup today, and I want you to keep an eye on their pitcher. His name is Eiji Sawamura, if I said that right. He's not much more than a kid, maybe seventeen or eighteen, and they say he's a phenom. See what you think, you know, not just how fast he pitches, but whether he's smart with his pitches. Does he manage the game?"

"That sounds like you want to sign him."

"Well, if he's even close to what I've heard, I sure want to talk to him. And, I could use your help on that, too. He doesn't speak a word of English."

Moe rubbed his chin and said, "So, if he comes to the majors, he's going to need someone to interpret for him during the games, like maybe a catcher. Am I reading that correctly?"

"Let's see if he's the real deal first. If he is, this could work out for all of us."

"I like the sound of that." He glanced at the pitcher's mound and said, "I'd better go. It's time to warm up."

* * * *

Moe had caught a sharp Lefty Gomez for six innings, when he took a seat on the bench and Connie Mack sat beside him. "What do you think, kid?"

"I assume you're asking my opinion of the boy wonder."

"Why else would I be here talking to you when our guys are coming to bat?"

"Yes, of course. Statistically speaking, he has struck out our best hitters, Ruth and Jimmie Foxx twice, and Gehrig once. The balls that have been hit have been less than impressive. We've trounced every Japanese team we've played, double-digit wins, but not today. If Lefty weren't throwing well, we could be in trouble in this game."

"He's awfully young. Do you think the pressure of the majors would break him down?"

"He didn't flinch when we had a runner on third with no outs. This looks like a tough-minded young man, but I'd like to talk with him, see what makes him click."

"Good, then we'll do that right after the game. Akito got permission from his manager, but, when it comes time to talk business, I don't want some foreigner translating what I say."

Two popups and a grounder punched out the Americans in the seventh, and the final two innings didn't take much longer. Mack and Berg waited for the other players to leave for the showers, and they crossed to the opposing dugout, where they found a thin, young man waiting. Moe bowed and said, "Thank you for agreeing to see us, and please excuse my poor use of your language."

"I am pleased to meet you, and your Japanese is very good. I have heard of you, the big man from America who taught our people the game I love."

"I can't take credit for teaching your people about baseball. I was here a couple of years ago, but most of my time was spent on the science of catching."

"You are too modest. What is it you wish to speak about?"

"This man is Connie Mack. He owns and manages the baseball team in Philadelphia. He is willing to pay you a lot of money to play baseball in the United States."

"That I cannot do."

"But, you haven't heard the offer yet. I assure you, Mr. Mack can be very generous."

"I will not go, because I hate America. The emperor has told us of the atrocities your government has committed against our people. Your ships block our trade routes, and our people suffer. You would make us your slaves, as you did the Africans. You show no honor."

"What's wrong, Moe? He looks upset."

"It isn't going well, Mr. Mack. These people believe what their leaders tell them, and they've been told a lot of bad things about us. The emperor's word is like the voice of God to them. Give me another minute." He turned back to Sawamura. "Eiji, I understand that you don't trust the American government, but will you trust me, as a man?"

"If I were to trust any American, it would be you, but I will not earn money in a country that treats my homeland with distain." He looked into Moe's eyes. "It saddens me that our nations are becoming enemies. If it were not so, I would be your friend."

"I understand, Eiji, and I hope, in better times, we will be friends." He put his hand on Mack's shoulder. "It's a no, Connie."

"No? I can make this kid rich. Tell him, Moe."

"He doesn't care about being rich. He cares about things that aren't so fashionable anymore. I'm glad I met him."

* * * *

Evening came with a cutting wind, the smell of humanity on the streets, and dinner at a familiar night club. "I'll be leaving after dinner, Babe" Moe said. "But, Akito will introduce you to the private entertainment room after I'm gone."

"Why can't I go there now?"

"You'll enjoy the experience better on a full stomach, assuming you ever have a full stomach."

"Go to hell, Berg. Oh, that reminds me, I'd like to try some of that green stuff the guy at the next table has."

Moe wagged his head with a smile, and his mind drifted to Eiji Sawamura. *He's so young and so committed. He's wrong about America, but he'll never know it, isolated on an island nation and buried in its propaganda. He loves his country as much as I love mine. Does loving your country always mean loving its government?* A squeal from the waitress brought him back to the present. "Come on, Babe, that's the third time you've run your hand under that girl's kimono."

"Yeah, you'd think she'd get the message by now."

Berg spoke to the girl in Japanese and then said, "She's married, so she's nervous about being touched, but she understands and she has something she'd like to say to you."

"How's she going to do that if she doesn't speak English?"

"I could translate, but it wouldn't be the same as hearing it from her." He took a slip of paper from his pocket and scribbled on it. "I'm writing the words phonetically, so she can bear her heart to you from her own lips."

"Okay, now we're getting somewhere."

Berg handled the note to the waitress. She read it, looked at the big man, and said, "Screw you, Babe Ruth."

* * * *

Moe hid the film he shot from the hospital in the lining of his suitcase. Then he went about Tokyo, filming everything in sight, but always storing those reels separate from his treasure. When the tour of games ended, he sailed to Korea and crossed into China by train. The Aktung Police caught him filming the Yalu River and seized his film, but not the reels in his suitcase. The Tran Siberian Railway brought him to Moscow and Red Square. Estella didn't meet him there, but a member of the Red Army did and confiscated his passport. Moe waited for hours in the snow, wondering how he would get out of Russia. Finally, the soldier returned and handed the passport back. And, Moe knew it was time to go home.

* * * *

Glenn Myatt's broken leg healed, and Cleveland gave Moe his full release. Somehow going home didn't feel right, so he boarded a train for New York. What were the chances of finding a girl he'd met only once and written but twice, and why would she want to see him? The questions didn't matter, only the answers. And, when it came to dinner at Leo Lindy's night club, the answer was yes.

Glasses of white burgundy and Chablis highlighted a table centered with cut flowers and covered by a white, linen cloth. Estella refused dessert and took her wine in hand. "So, you said they took your film on the train, and then you went to Moscow. It occurs to me that this loss of film takes away any real evidence that you travelled to any of these places."

"And, I lost more in Russia. They're building a subway, but all the work is masked by wooden barriers. I pulled one of them down, and who do you suppose they had put to work, outdoors, in the dead of winter?"

"Let me guess. Trained gorillas riding donkeys."

"Women. They were all women, working in sub-zero temperatures, swinging picks to break up frozen clods of dirt."

"Why do you find that offensive? Women are capable of physically-demanding work."

"Digging in dirt that's as hard as concrete, when it's twenty below, women's suffrage notwithstanding, is no job for a woman."

"It's probably no job for a man either. Did you film it?"

"Yes, but they caught me. A couple of plain-clothed policemen relived me of my camera, and a soldier took my passport." He lifted his glass and said, "So, I return to you with no cinematic evidence of my trip beyond the two reels I shot in Tokyo."

"And, just when do I get to see that at the movie theater?"

"I'm afraid Bugs Bunny and Popeye are under no immediate threat of being displaced by stunning footage shot from the top of Saint Luke's Hospital. My friend, Mr. Treadwell, whom I may have overestimated, seems to have disappeared. But, I do have the film in my hotel room, if you'd like to see it. Do you have a projector?"

"That sounds like a man inviting himself to my apartment." She took a drink of wine, and he said nothing. "In fact, I do have a projector, left over from the music school, but I'm not sure I should trust a man of your reputation under my roof. Will you behave?"

"That I cannot promise."

* * * *

Her modest flat spanned enough space for a kitchenette, bathroom, small bedroom, and a living room just large enough for her piano, a sofa, and one chair. Moe nestled close to her, but kept his hands in his lap. "I'm afraid the film is a little shaky at this point, but it gets better."

"It must've been cold and windy on top of the hospital."

"Yes, oh, here is the harbor. I love this view. You can see the Sea of Japan. That's the Imperial Palace in the distance. Magnificent. And, well, that's a factory and, again, another factory." He stopped the projector and said, "That's really all that's worth seeing. The rest is mundane, government buildings and the like." He pulled one knee onto the cushion between them. "I'd love to go back, and I wish you'd come with me."

"Aren't you getting a bit ahead of yourself, Moe? Most men would find a job before planning another trip around the world."

"I think I have one. Joe Cronin is an old teammate of mine, and he's managing the Red Sox. I'd be a backup again, but he has a new kid he asked me to mentor."

"He wants you to mentor a young catcher to take your job?"

"Not a catcher. This boy is only a year out of high school. He's a power hitter, but he has trouble with breaking balls, like most young guys do when they get to the majors. His name is Ted Williams. Joe showed me film of him hitting in San Diego. Once he understands how to read a pitch, he could do some terrific things at the plate."

"You make him sound like Rogers Hornsby."

"He could be better than Hornsby. His swing is as pure as Shoeless Joe's. And, the job's in Boston, only two hundred miles from here. You could come up for games, just take the express to Hartford and then on to Boston."

"I'd like that. Now, it's after eleven. If we want to avoid a scandal, you'd better go."

He took her hand. "I'd hoped to stay."

"I'm not some flapper, Moe, and I never will be. I could live with the separation, weekends together, until your playing days are over, but I must be the only one. I won't share you."

"I don't want to be shared, not anymore. I've been something of a nomad, I'm afraid, and I don't know if I can change that. But, I will never cheat on you. Never." He fumbled for words, and then said, "I can't say that I'm the type who gets married."

"Who said anything about getting married? You assume too much, Mr. Berg." She stood, pulled him to his feet, and took him to her bed.

Chapter Four

Moe and Estella's romance grew deeper with time, as did their passion for each other. They travelled between Boston and New York so often that porters came to call them by name. Moe spent the off season in her apartment, to the chagrin of her neighbors. Then came their greatest test, the trip home. Newark never felt as cold and uninviting as it did in January 1939. Moe sat in the back of the taxi with one foot propped on the hump in the floor and the other stretched under the driver's seat. He groaned as the cab turned the corner and his parents' house came into view. "Okay, Stella, this is it. I hope you're not disappointed."

"You worry too much, Moe. I'm sure they'll be lovely. We're not living in the 19th Century anymore." The car rolled to a stop by the curb, they each retrieved one bag from the truck, and Moe's I'm-back-home headache appeared in his forehead.

When they reached the porch, they didn't need to knock. The door swung open, and Ethel stepped out. "You must be Estella. I'm Ethel, Moe's big sister." Stella took her hand, thanked her for her courtesy, and followed her inside. "You can leave your bags by the sofa for now. Mama has a room for you upstairs and one for Moe next to the kitchen."

"Moe and I won't need separate rooms."

"You will here. Trust me. Well, speak of the devil. The lady bursting through the kitchen door in the apron is our mother."

Rose scurried into the room, hugged them both warmly, and said, "Moe, where are your manners? Take her coat."

"We just walked in the door, Mama. I haven't . . ."

"Oh, let me look at her. Yes, a lovely girl. A little skinny, but we'll fix that with some dinner. Ah, Moe, it's your favorite, lamb and potatoes and raspberries."

"Lamb isn't my favorite."

Estella pulled off her coat and handed it to Moe. "Never argue with you mother. Mrs. Berg, is there somewhere I could freshen up? We've had a long trip."

She pointed to the hallway. "Down to the end, on the left. Dinner should be ready in a few minutes."

Moe hung their coats in the closet and turned back to his mother, but she was gone. "She doesn't really expect Stella and me to sleep in separate rooms, does she, Ethel?"

"Not Mama. It's him."

"Yeah, where is he?"

"Papa's in his bedroom and won't come down. Personally, I think Estella may be the most beautiful and refined woman I've ever met, but he says he's not going to meet the woman who's living out of wedlock with his son." Moe stormed up the stairs with his sister calling after him. "He won't talk to you. I tried."

The floor creaked under his heavy steps, as Moe reached the bedroom door and snatched it open. He saw his father sitting by the window reading, and the boy he once was arose, draining the rage from his voice. "Papa, I'd like to talk to you."

Bernard kept reading and said, "You've forgotten how to knock on a door before you come in?"

"I didn't come to talk about manners, and you know that." He stepped closer and sat on the edge of the bed. "I want to know why you're not coming down to meet Stella."

The old man lowered his book and carefully plucked the glasses from his nose. "You live with a woman who is not your wife, a woman who is not of your faith, and you wonder why I don't take her to my breast and welcome her to ruin my son's life?"

"And, since when have you been so high on being a Jew? You live in a Protestant neighborhood, and you almost never go to the synagogue. I'm more of a Jew than you ever were."

"Our blood runs pure for thousands of years, and now you would mix it with a Christian? No, I tell you. I will not bring a shiksa into this family."

"Be careful, Papa. Stella is important to me, more important than any woman I've known, and I won't have you talking down about her."

"Important? She is only important to you because she will take you to her bed. She lies with you and is not married to you. It is shameful, and what happens when she is with child? Will you marry this woman?"

"I just might." Moe rubbed his eyes and thought about what his father had said. Marriage? He'd always been free to do as he pleased, succeed or fail without worrying about anyone else. But, now he wanted something more. "The problem is that she won't marry me, at least not yet. Papa, I've bounced from one city to another, one team to another, playing baseball, and I love it. I've travelled from Paris to Egypt to China, all over the world. That's not the life of a family man. I know it, and so does she. I'm trying to change, but I don't know if I can."

Bernard set his book on the window sill and took his son's hand. "You're a good man, Moe, and you know what is right. Rid yourself of this woman."

Moe pushed his father's hand away and stood. "This woman? You won't even call her name. It's Stella, and she's dearer to me than life itself. If she is not welcome in your home, then neither am I. Now, I'm going to have dinner with my family. If you don't come down before we leave, then we have spoken our last words."

As he stepped into the hallway, Moe heard his father call to him. "Close the door."

* * * *

February came with an arctic blast, the coldest Moe could remember. Was it really that cold or was it just the fact that he was now thirty-seven years old, and it felt colder? Spring training waited in a few weeks, and he would warm himself in the gulf breezes of Sarasota, but only if the Red Sox still needed him. His time as a player was fading, and he knew it, but his popularity had never been higher. Stella followed him onto the elevator, waited for a moment, and then nudged him. "Which floor, Moe?"

He looked at her and then the elevator operator. "Oh, I'm not sure. The show is *Information Please*." The operator nodded and put the car in motion. "We'll find a chair when we get to the studio, and you can sit next to me, Stella."

"No, no, I just came to watch. I can sit with the audience."

"Okay, but try to sit where I can see you. This is my first time on the program, and I'm a little nervous."

"You, the guy with a photographic memory, nervous about a quiz show?"

"People mail in the questions. They could be about anything. What if they ask me a question about farming or something?"

"Pass it off to one of the other panelists. There are two others, right?" The elevator stopped, the doors opened, and she tugged on his coat. "Come on, Nervous Nelly, let's get you in there." They checked in with the receptionist and passed through a set of double doors emblazoned with the letters *NBC Radio*. Stella slipped her hand into the crook of his elbow. "Well, you should have some help on current events. The guy at the end of the table is Oscar Levant, the newspaper columnist."

"Yes, I've met him before."

"Is that other guy who I think he is?"

"If you think he's Boris Karloff, then yes. The man who gave us nightmares, in the flesh."

"He looks so different without the monster makeup. Kind of handsome, in a rugged sort of way."

"Okay, enough of that. Go find yourself a place to sit before the electrodes pop out of his neck, and you are hopelessly seduced by his charm." Moe took his seat, nodded to Levant, and said, "Hello, Mr. Karloff."

"Gooood Eeeeving."

"Somehow I knew you'd say that."

Karloff smiled. "People expect it. And, it's one of the reasons I agreed to do this program. I'd like for them to see me as more than the character on the movie screen."

And, with that, the broadcast started. "Hello, everyone. This is Clifton Fadiman, your host for *Information Please*, the program that lets you, the listener, challenge our panel of experts to answer questions about any subject you choose. Tonight's broadcast is brought to you by Lucky Strike. Remember, L.S.M.F.T, Lucky Strike Means Fine Tobacco. And, now let me introduce our panel of experts. To my far left is one of our regulars, renowned columnist and musical aficionado, Mr. Oscar Levant. Now, Oscar, many of our listeners know you for composing the very popular song, *Blame It On My Youth*. Are you feeling youthful tonight?"

"I'm ready, Clift. I'm afraid the radio audience isn't going to win much money on me tonight."

"Well, the challenge is out there, folks. Now, please give a warm welcome to a man who needs no introduction, Mr. Boris Karloff." A round of applause rose from the studio audience, and Karloff bobbed his head. "Boris, did you get a jolt of electricity to spark those brain waves today?"

Karloff shrugged. "I will do my best."

"And, now we have a newcomer. You've heard about this man, a catcher with the Boston Red Sox, affectionately known as the Professor. Folks, this guy has a string of degrees long enough to hang yourself on. Ladies and gentlemen, Moe Berg." He waited for a modest applause to end and said, "Our first question comes from Des Moines, and we'll start with the newest member of our panel. Moe, Molly Wilson wants to know which one of our presidents played sports while in college."

"The question is wrong, Clift."

"I'm sorry, did you say the question is wrong?"

"Yes, it implies that only one president played collegiate sports. Theodore Roosevelt was a boxer, and President Wilson played baseball at Princeton. Warren Harding didn't actually play sports, but he did work as a sports writer for a time."

"And, there you have it folks. Professor Berg not only answers the question, he expands on it. Nicely done, Moe."

The show ran for thirty minutes, with occasional interruptions to advertise cigarettes and Octagon soap, and Berg answered every question put to him. As he and Stella shuffled past the receptionist, she stopped him. "Excuse me, are you Mr. Berg?"

"Yes."

"I have a call for you." She handed him the telephone receiver.

"Hello, this is Moe Berg. Who is this?"

"Boy, this is Kennesaw Mountain Landis. I've been listening to the show, and I couldn't be more pleased."

"Well, thank you, sir."

"You did more for baseball in thirty minutes than I've done in my entire career as commissioner. Keep it up, son."

"Yes, sir, I'll try." He dropped the receiver onto the cradle and turned to Stella with a crooked grin. "Wow. That was Commissioner Landis. He was listening, and he was very pleased. Maybe he'll help me get another year with the Red Sox. Can you wait a year for me to settle down, Stell?"

"Don't make a promise you can't keep, Moe. Are you saying you'll be finished with baseball in another year?"

"I think baseball might be finished with me."

* * * *

The Red Sox were not finished with Moe Berg, not yet, and the year he promised Stella stretched to two. He spent most of the summer warming up relief pitchers in the bullpen and expounding to batters on his theories of how to calculate what pitch will be thrown next. In the middle of August, he faced the Washington Senators and sat on the bullpen bench, strapping on his shin guards. He wondered why no one else had come to the bullpen yet, and the answer came wrapped in a tweed suit. "Hello, Moe. Do you remember me?"

"Treadwell, isn't it? I thought you had vanished into the mist."

"Not entirely. I apologize for not following up with you on your film of Tokyo, but I've been on assignment in Europe."

"Keeping an eye on the Fuerher?"

"I can't say, but Hitler may be a threat to us."

"How can you say that? *Time Magazine* named him Man of the Year only two years ago. Has he fallen from grace so quickly?"

"Hitler took Poland last year, and he invaded France three months ago. He won't stop there. Another war is brewing, Moe."

"That may be true, but how does that affect us. We have an ocean between us and Europe. They'd have to build a rocket as tall as a skyscraper to carry enough fuel to reach us. They don't have the technology or the resources to do that. It's a fantasy, Buck Rogers."

"They may not have to cross the ocean. The President asked Nelson Rockefeller to organize a group to collect intelligence on German influence in Central and South America. If the Nazis get a toehold in Panama or even Brazil, they could build their weapons and march right to our doorstep."

Berg stood and wedged his catcher's mask under his arm. "Why are you telling me all this? I'm a baseball player."

"President Roosevelt has heard of you. He knows about your language skills, your acumen, and your love of country. We'd give you a cover story. You went to Japan twice to teach their athletes. We could say you're visiting our military bases to build morale through sports. When you're not with the troops, you gather intelligence."

"That's you plan? You guys are new at this, aren't you?"

"We're learning. We have people in London right now, working with MI6. The Brits have been spying on other countries for centuries. Your country needs you, Moe. Will you help her?"

"You asked that before I left for Japan and, when I got back with the film, you were gone. That makes me wary of you, Mr. Treadwell. Having said that, if America were under threat, I'd sign up today, but she isn't. I have plans for my life, a girl for goodness sake. The Red Sox gave me a job coaching. I have obligations." His words rang strange in his own ears. Obligations? Promises? Was he really saying those things? "As long as the trouble stays in Europe, I stay out of it."

"Is that your final word on it?"

"It is, but, should Hitler ever build that giant rocket, come and see me again."

"Very well, Mr. Berg, but I may be back sooner than you think."

"That isn't likely. Grab yourself a hotdog and stay for the game. We're pitching Lefty Grove today. I expect to win."

* * * *

Berg carried Treadwell's words with him through the week, even to the train station where he met Stella on Friday evening. They crawled through his brain like worms eating their way into his conscience, until he reached his hotel and sat down for dinner. It was time to put them aside and concentrate on the woman in his life. She was as elegant as ever, a pearl necklace draped around her neck, deep brown eyes, and a smile that spoke to the deepest parts of his soul.

As they took their table, a stocky, curly-haired man brushed past and said, "How you doing, Moe?"

"Oh, hi, Lenny. I'm doing well. Give my best to your brothers."

Stella watched the man leave and asked, "I've seen that guy."

"His name is Leonard. I call him Lenny, but, when he's in character, most people know him as Chico."

"How do you know Chico Marx?"

"I've known the Marx brothers for probably five or six years. They like coming to the ball games. Well, I don't know all of them. I never met Zeppo or Gummo." The sound of laughter drew his attention to the door. "Oh, great. It's the guys from the team."

"Invite them over. I'd like to meet them."

"I don't know. They're not exactly your type. Maybe they won't see us."

But, they did, and Jimmie Foxx yelled across the dining room. "Hey, look over there. It's the Professor, and he's got a dame with him." The trio of ballplayers stumbled between tables until they stood around Moe. They pulled spare chairs from other tables and sat without being invited. "Say, Moe, who's your friend?"

"Gentlemen, this is the Countess Astoria of Romania. I'm afraid she speaks no English and is visiting for only a few days." The players looked at each other, and Stella offered her hand. "Fellows, it's customary to stand and kiss the hand of royalty."

Foxx clamored to his feet. "Yeah, yeah, we were just about to do that." He bowed, kissed the back of Stella's gloved hand, and said, "I'm very happy to make your acquaintance, ma'am." He sat down and muttered, "All right, you guys." And, the other two followed suit. "I never met a countess before. Ask her how she likes America, Moe. Does she like baseball?"

"Romanian is not my strongest language, so we communicate in German." He forced back a grin and said, "Have you had enough of these guys yet?"

"I think we should have some sport with them. Tell him that I'm offended by his jacket."

"Jimmie, she says you're wearing the same plaid as the tribe that raided her village when she was a girl. She finds it very offensive."

"Really? Well, hell, I'll take it off then." He pulled off the jacket and folded it over the back of his chair.

Moe and Stella exchanged words in German again, and Moe turned back to Foxx. "She says the pants are the same plaid and that you must've been sent here to embarrass her. This isn't good, Jimmie. We could be looking at an international incident here."

"Well, I ain't taking my pants off. I'll leave if she wants, but the pants stay on."

"It's too late for leaving. This is her first visit to America. Our ambassador has been trying to forge an alliance with Romania, and the first thing we do is rub her nose in the very symbol she has grown to hate. If you are a real American, you'll kick those pants off."

Foxx sat for a moment, his gaze traversing the table, from one person to another. "Well, nobody says I'm not an American." He unclipped his suspenders, unsnapped the waist, and slid his trousers off, as he sat in his chair. "Is she happy now?"

"What shall I tell him, Madame Countess? Is this enough?"

Stella pursed her lips and spoke in English. "Them is some jam-up gams you've got there, mug. Did you get them off a mannequin at Macy's?"

"Berg, you are a son of a bitch." Foxx yanked his pants over his legs, grabbed the jacket from his chair, and pointed at Moe. "Damn it, Moe. Leave me bare-assed in front of all these people. If I wasn't . . ." Then he laughed. "Hell, you got me. I'd have done it to you, if I had the chance. Come on, boys, let's get out of here before some cop takes me to jail."

They left in the same bawdy fashion as they had entered. Stella watched them go and said, "You love those guys, don't you."

"Oh, they're okay, I guess."

"What's wrong, Moe. You look troubled."

"A guy came to see me today, a government man. They want me to go to South America to see what's up with the Nazis there."

"You're not actually considering it, are you?"

"I don't know. Europe is in flames, Stell. All over the continent men, women, and children are dying, while I'm sitting in the bullpen telling jokes to the pitchers. Soon, we'll be in the middle of it. We can't deny that for long."

"But, you're a ballplayer, a scholar. War is not your business."

"Maybe it is. Maybe it is exactly my business." He raised his glass. "Let's drink to peace while we can."

* * * *

His leather heels clicked on the tile floors of the Commerce Building, as Berg made his way to a door marked *Office of Inter-American Affairs*. He hung his hat on top of the coat rack, and the receptionist led him to a small conference room, where three men sat around a square table. "Ah, Moe, I'm glad you could make it. Please have a seat."

"Good morning, Mr. Rockefeller."

"Please shake hands with John Clark, my director, and I think you know Mr. Treadwell."

"Mr. Clark, nice to meet you. Mr. Treadwell."

Rockefeller propped both elbows on the table and said, "Let me put things into perspective. I report directly to President Roosevelt, so we have support at the highest levels of government. I would not have accepted this appointment under any other conditions. My operational view is from ten-thousand feet. Mr. Clark handles the daily specifics of our work, so I'll step aside and let him speak for the department. He would be your primary contact for the future."

"Thank you, sir. Let me get straight to the point. Moe, have you considered our offer?"

"First, gentlemen, thank you for inviting me. I've given your proposition a lot of thought. In reviewing the eco-political environment in both Central and South America, I believe we would be better served to start in Costa Rica, as a diversion, and move quickly to Brazil. Getulio Vargas is a dictator of some renown, perhaps brutal, but we need to get to him before the Nazis do."

"That sounds like you'll be joining us."

"Oh, yes, yes. I'll need a few weeks to tie up my loose ends, resign my coaching job with the Red Sox and the like, and I do have a few requirements."

"What kind of requirements?"

"If I am to gather meaningful intelligence, then I'll need access to people of rank and influence. I cannot entertain men of that caliber in fleabag hotels. I'll need funding for the best accommodations and ready cash to pay for information. Bribery is distasteful to most Americans, but it is a way of life in countries like Brazil."

Clark scribbled a few notes on a pad and then looked up. "We would expect a sizable return on our investment, if we give you all you ask."

"And, you'll get it. I mean no disrespect to you or Mr. Rockefeller, but it's important that we speak frankly. The United States has no meaningful experience in gathering military intelligence, especially in times of peace. We have no in-house experts upon whom to call for advice. And, we're not likely to employ torture like the Gestapo, nor should we. If we are to drain information from high-level Nazi officials, we are left with an approach that says we cajole those we can and bribe the rest. Either option calls for money."

"I won't deny that we are plowing new ground here, but we are in touch with MI6 to train our agents. They've been less than forthcoming, since we are yet to join the war, but we do believe they have an agent in Brazil. We just don't know who it is." He tapped his pencil on the table. "You'll be facing the Abwehr, Germany's version of military intelligence. They are led by an Admiral Canaris, a tough customer, and he has a head start on us with the locals. Moe, you do understand that, if you try to bribe Nazi officials, and they don't bite, they're probably going to murder you. Do you get that?"

"Of course. And, in that event, the ballgame changes."

"Are you prepared to kill or to die?"

"Let's hope it doesn't come to that. If it does, then I will have failed, and I don't plan to fail."

* * * *

Most of the passengers on Berg's flight had fallen to sleep under the constant drone of the propellers, but not Moe. His black suit and tie had given way to khaki pants and a white shirt. He sat alone, submitting to memory the details of a dossier for Wilhelm Canaris, and he muttered as he read, "Let's see, decorated veteran of the Great War, reports to the High Command. Hmm, he takes occasional trips to Spain, could be on the outs with Himmler. Maybe I can use that." It was like scouting an opposing pitcher before a big game, but this time he had to destroy the scouting report. When he finished, he walked to the restroom, removed the papers from the folder, and tore them to tiny bits before burning them in the sink.

He returned to his seat in time for the final approach. As the plane circled Rio de Janeiro, it passed by the statue of Christ the Redeemer, standing nearly a hundred feet tall atop Cordova Mountain, its arms outstretched over a land on the verge of falling to Nazi influence. The tires squealed twice before settling into a taxi for the gate. Berg collected his bags and took a taxi to his hotel. As he signed the guest book, he noticed two men in black uniforms. "Are you Morris Berg?" one asked.

"Yes, and who might you be, other than Gestapo?"

"Our names are not important. You will come with us."

"You seem to leave me little choice. Where are we going?"

"That you will learn when we get there."

Moe turned to the desk clerk. "Would you have my luggage taken to my room? I hope to return for it." He walked between the two officers to a long, black car and rode several blocks to a building that bore a Nazi flag at its entrance. Moe had never felt as uneasy as he did passing through those doors. On the third floor, his escorts released him to a short, portly man wearing round glasses over an equally round nose. "I am Colonel Shneider. Come this way, the admiral is waiting." They walked to the end of the hall, where oak doors opened to an elegant office of mahogany furniture, centered by a large desk and leather seats. The doors closed with an ominous click. "Mr. Berg, this is Admiral Canaris, head of Abwehr Intelligence."

"Good afternoon, Admiral. To what do I owe this pleasure?"

"We will discuss that in a moment. Please have a seat."

"Thank you."

"Would you like a cigar?"

"I generally don't smoke, unless smoking cigars is meant as a punishment." Neither German even cracked a smile. "Perhaps my humor would translate better in German?"

"Well, Mr. Berg, you make no pretense of your language skills. A man who speaks numerous languages and who has no wife or family ties, he would make the perfect spy."

"Since you had your people pick me up so quickly, then I assume you know everything about me, including my affinity for language. Why should I deny what you already know? But, I am no spy, just a baseball player who is growing too old to play the game much longer."

Canaris' voice grew stern. "I know that you are a Jew, the son of Jews who fled the Ukraine. You graduated first in your class from Princeton and have a law degree from Columbia University. You came here from Costa Rica, where you spent two months and flew your mistress there for three weekends. You speak my language almost as well as your own, and you work for the United States government. What is your assignment here, Mr. Berg?"

"Strictly to improve the morale of our soldiers through sports and good health."

"Will you teach them your sport of baseball?"

"They already know how to play baseball, Admiral. You know that. I came to organize their sporting events, to help them get the equipment they need, and to show them how to improve their health. Part of that is to deter them from unhealthy practices, such as prostitution, and, in failing that, to encourage the use of condoms to prevent disease."

Canaris pounded his fist on the desk. "You are lying. You came here to spy. I could have you shot." He bounded to his feet, yelling. "I could kill you here and now, and have your body taken to the ocean and fed to the crabs." He put his hand on the grip of his Luger. "Don't test me, Mr. Berg. What is your assignment?"

It was the first time Moe's life had been threatened, and from someone who could do exactly what he said he would do. But, he answered calmly. "My assignment is as I told you, to promote health and fitness among American troops. Perhaps you should save your bullets for someone more deserving and spare the crabs a meal they may not like."

Canaris turned to Schneider. "Get this Jew out of my office. He fouls the air I breathe."

Schneider saluted, took Moe's elbow, and pulled him from the chair. "You will come with me."

Moe's legs were weak, but they carried him to the door and down the hall. "Will your two gentlemen be giving me a ride back to my hotel?"

"Yes. You will stay with me until they arrive."

"Oh, good. I get so lonely when I ride alone."

"Perhaps you will not be so coy, when the entire world speaks German."

"That day will never come, not now, not ever."

* * * *

Berg knew Adwehr agents were watching him and he needed to maintain at least the appearance of a cover, so he took a cab to the brothel nearest the American Army base. Scattered bricks covered the holes in its rusty, tin roof, and a rancid odor greeted him at the open entrance. A stout, middle-aged woman waited inside. "Brunette or redhead?" she asked.

Moe flashed his identification and said, "Do you have American soldiers here?"

"No, I am just a sick woman with a boarding house. Americans don't stay here."

"I'm not here to cause you trouble. I only want to talk to them." He pressed two hundred cruzeiros in her palm. Then he gripped her wrist tightly. "I'm going to ask you nicely one more time. Do you have any American soldiers here?"

"Only the one, at the top of the stairs on the left, but he is very drunk."

"Thank you." He clattered up the steps to the second floor, and the odor was worse, with the smell of heavy perfume and soiled linens left unwashed. He entered the room without knocking and found a lieutenant sprawled over a narrow bed with a young woman straddling his hips. He motioned to the girl. "Get out. Get out now!" She didn't ask why, but just slid off the bed, closed her gown, and scampered out. Berg rolled the soldier over and slapped his face.

"What the hell? You son of a . . ."

"Don't finish that sentence, soldier. You'll regret it if you do." The man rubbed his face and reached for a bottle of gin on the bedside table, but Berg got to it first. "You've had enough of that, but I wouldn't mind a drink. I've had a full morning." He took two full gulps and poured the rest onto the floor.

"Shit, what are you doing? That's good stuff." He pulled himself up, his back resting against the wall, and cross buttoned his wrinkled shirt. "This ain't right. I get one day off, and some guy dumps my gin and runs my girl off."

"What was her name?"

"Whose name?"

"Your girl. You said I ran your girl off, and I'd like to know her name."

"Uh, Angelina or Conchitta or something like that. Hell, how am I supposed to know? I'm drunk."

"Then, what's your name?"

The soldier grinned. "Now, that I know. My name is Max Carson, Lieutenant Max Carson at your service."

"And, what are you doing in Brazil, Max Carson?"

Carson recited his answer like he had said it a hundred times. "Training, sir. I am an American soldier, training and providing services to the people of Brazil, while waiting for assignment to an undetermined location." And, he laughed.

"I don't think you're as drunk as you want me to believe. If you are, then you've done a good job of parroting the company line. But, you are a disgrace, and an officer to boot. Now, get out of that bed."

"I like it here." Berg grabbed the front of his shirt, snatched him to his feet, and dragged him into the bathtub. When the cold water hit Carson's body, he squealed like an Alpine yodeler. "Ooowee, you asshole. Damn, that is some bad shit."

Berg turned off the water and tossed him a dingy towel. "Dry yourself off. We've got things to do."

The towel muffled his voice as Carson answered. "What kind of things?"

"That's the clearest thing you've said yet. Maybe you're not so drunk."

"Well, I ain't feeling no pain, but, like you said, I am an officer. That's why I come here in the middle of the day, so the enlisted men won't see me acting this way. I'm not the bum you think I am."

"And, you're not regular Army either. You're OSS."

"Hell, mister, I don't even know what that is."

"Oh, you know. I read your file before I left Washington. Max Carson, first lieutenant, born in Michigan, I believe."

"You seem to know a lot about me." He pushed off the wall and rose to his feet. "So, who are you?"

"Don't worry about who I am for now. Straighten yourself up. You're going to drive me to the base."

"You nearly drown me just to get a ride? Why don't you drive yourself?"

"I don't drive, but that's not your worry. Your clothes can dry on the ride. Where is your Jeep, Max?"

"It's a block up the street, parked in front of the bank."

Moe wrapped Carson's tie around his neck and plopped his cap onto his head. "There, you look great. I need to look busy, so let's go.

* * * *

A twenty minute drive in the open air did dry Carson's uniform, and still Berg didn't tell him who he was, not even when he showed his credentials at the gate. "Take me to your men first, Max. I have a whiz-bang speech about living a healthy lifestyle and a pocket full of condoms to pass out."

"Condoms? Say, I could probably use a few of those."

"Yes, I don't suppose Angelina or Conchitta, or whatever her name might be, provides those to her customers, does she?"

"Well, she sure doesn't provide them for me, but that's about all she doesn't do." He navigated between three sets of barracks until he reached a small hut set between two tall trees. "There she is, home sweet home. There are only a half dozen of us. You had me pegged right as OSS, but you know that. They keep us separated from the regular soldiers to keep the new guys from saying something they shouldn't say in front of the wrong person. Let's walk around to the back. The guys are probably playing ball this time of day."

"Baseball?"

"Yeah, do you play?"

"I played some in college." As they rounded the back corner of the hut, Berg caught sight of three men tossing a baseball between them in a triangle. Watching them play felt warm, familiar. It reminded him of home and Stella. He heard one of the men curse when he missed the ball, and it rolled to Berg's feet.

"How about a little help there, buddy?" The man said. Moe picked it up, shifted his feet, and fired it back. The man caught it and said, "You're a catcher." Moe didn't answer, and he tossed it back. Moe rolled the ball in his hands, flipped it in the air, and fired a strike, like gunning down a runner at second base. Again, the man caught it. "Whoa, that had some heat. You're a professional." He paused. "And, your name is Moe Berg."

"Well, Max, it looks like I'm going to need to be more careful. People seem to find me out too easily."

* * * *

Evening came early in a city nestled between mountains, and Moe Berg took the elevator down to the hotel lobby with a bundle of newspapers under his arm. He had hardly noticed the woman standing beside him until she spoke in whispered Portuguese. "Do not eat in the hotel dining room."

"I'm sorry. Were you speaking to me?"

"You will walk directly through the dining room into the kitchen and leave through the back door. I will meet you in the alley." The doors opened, and she was gone.

Berg walked into the dining room, found a table, and stacked his newspapers on top. He ordered a glass of wine and asked the waiter for directions to the restroom. Before reaching the restroom, he turned into the kitchen, as if by accident. The rattle of pans and utensils filled his ears, as he brushed past and out the door. A single light bulb kept the alley from complete darkness. The woman's voice called from a waiting car, this time in English with a very British accent. "Get in." Berg took a step closer and stopped. "Quickly, before they find us."

His quick steps echoed down the alley, he hurried into the car, and they sped away. "All right, I am in a car with a strange woman, being ferried away, and I don't know who you are or where we're going."

"I am your contact with MI6. You may call me Lydia."

"I am very happy to meet you, Lydia, and you may call me Moe. If I am to ride off with you, I should like to hear your last name."

"Farmington."

"Lydia Farmington. It has the ring of an alias, but you are a very attractive lady, so I'll not press you for more. Does MI6 have many black agents like you?"

"That's classified information."

"Naturally, it would be. Now, with the introductions complete, what the hell is going on here?"

"Your mission in Brazil is taking a turn, a very significant turn, one your government does not understand yet. Is anyone following us?"

"Uh, let's see. No, I don't see any headlights." She turned sharply down a narrow street to the left. "I suppose you don't believe me."

"Keep watching. See whether a car passes under the street light behind us. They may be running without lights."

"I don't see, you're a very good driver, by the way. No, no other cars."

"Good, it appears we have lost compellingthe guards who were watching you. The Abwehr is incompetent, but we have to be careful."

"Incompetent? They knew almost everything about me."

"That's because I told them. It was necessary." She turned right.

"Well, I hope 'necessary' doesn't get me shot and fed to the crabs. Where are we going?"

"To a villa outside the city, perhaps twenty minutes. Try to relax. Do you have a gun?"

"You tell me to relax and then ask whether I have a gun. Do you see the irony in that? Never mind. No, I don't have a weapon. I'm sure the Nazis searched my bags while I was with Admiral Canaris, and a gun would've made them even more suspicious. Besides, I'm not an assassin."

"Look in the glove box. Yes, there. Put it in your pocket."

"Since when does British Intelligence carry snub-nose thirty-eights?"

"You will find it easy to conceal, but it is only accurate at close range. If you have to use it, shoot to kill. The Nazis don't give second chances. We've talked enough for now. Please keep watch out the back windshield. I'll explain everything when we arrive." The highway narrowed as they entered the countryside and wound into the hills. They turned onto a steep, dirt road and followed it to a set of open, iron gates. Lydia parked the car behind a shed and bade him follow her through a copse of trees to a garden, lit only by the night skies, to a man seated on a bench.

"I see you made it safely, Mr. Berg."

"Admiral Canaris?" He slipped his hand into his pocket. "What kind of trick is this?"

"You won't need your pistol. Please have a seat and let me explain." Moe eased onto a bench, facing Canaris, with Lydia beside him. "I hope you will accept my apologies for being so rude to you today, but it was necessary. You see, I must publically represent the Reich in unrelenting fashion, especially when Colonel Schneider is present. I suspect he was sent here to monitor my behavior on behalf of our Minster of the Interior. It seems Heir Himmler does not trust me."

"I can understand why you would be cautious. Are you telling me you want to defect to the United States?"

"Hardly. I am a German and will always be German, but I cannot, in good conscience, support the Fuhrer. How much does your government know of the atrocities in Poland?"

"That I could not say."

"Then, let me tell you. Following the Great War, my country was in shambles, our economy devastated. Hitler came to power with a promise to return Germany to greatness, and he blamed the economic problems on the Jews. They had fared well, many owned banks and flourished in a time when the populous, as a whole, did not. Hitler needed a target, and it came in the form of the Jews."

"That isn't an unusual way for a person to grab political power, but the United States would not see the taking of property as an atrocity. "

"But, it is more, Mr. Berg, much more. Jews all over Poland are being herded like cattle and murdered by the thousands, their bodies thrown into mass graves to be burned. If nothing is done, the numbers could reach millions. I tried to protest, but my superiors warned me against it. The order comes from Hitler himself."

"I mean no disrespect, Admiral, but that sounds a little fantastic."

"Listen to him, Moe," Lydia said. "Our sources in Poland tell us this is true."

He dug his fingers into his hair and said, "Americans abhor genocide, but what are we to do? The United States has not entered the war."

Canaris put his hand on Berg's knee. "But, you must. Our armies have marched over Austria, Poland, and now France with no meaningful resistance, but that is not enough for Hitler. He attacks England before we have even subdued the other nations."

"But, England is strong. He won't defeat them. You just said he has his hands full trying to hold onto what he's already taken."

"Are you familiar with Otto Hahn?"

"Yes, the German physicist. He claims to have split, no, that can't be."

Again, Lydia interrupted. "I'm afraid it is true. Hahn is working on fission as we speak, and the Nazis are forcing the most notable scientists in Italy and Germany to help him. They even have Werner Heisenberg on the project. Once they develop a bomb, they'll drop it on London and end the war in Europe. With footholds in South America, like Brazil, how long do you think it will take them to work their way up to Mexico and drop one on New York or Washington?"

"Whoa, that's a lot to swallow in one sitting. I know Czechoslovakia has uranium mines, and there's talk of heavy water factories. So, assuming this is true, what can we do to stop it?"

"Admiral?"

"We need America to enter the war effort now, not after the bomb has been developed. Her presence will bring a chilling effect on the High Command. They are not foolish men. There are plans in the works to assassinate Hitler, but I am looking for assurances from the United States that, once he is gone, the Allies will negotiate a truce that names me as the leader of the new Germany."

Berg stood and paced around the garden. Then he turned back to Canaris. "Admiral, ours is a political society. The President is not a dictator. He can't take us into a war without the consent of Congress, and he won't get that without proof of a direct threat on the United States. That threat only exists if there is a realistic opportunity for Germany to develop this weapon, and they have the means to deliver it against our cities. You say that could come through a partnership with someone like Brazil. If I go back whistling that tune without proof, they'll kick my butt onto the street."

"Then we shall get you proof, but it will be dangerous. Would you be willing to take a risk, perhaps risk your life?"

"Well, what do you have in mind?"

Canaris stood and raised an ear to the night. "I must go. Lydia, perhaps you would explain our plan to our new friend."

She nodded, and he stepped out of sight. "We have been working with Admiral Canaris for some time."

"Is that why he goes to Spain?"

"Is it that obvious? We need to be more careful. But, for the present, there is a valise in the car, and in that valise you will find a German uniform, an SS uniform. It should fit you. In the right pocket are papers that identify you as Heinrich Berger, a captain and envoy from the German High Command. You have been sent here to personally confirm Brazil's allegiance with the Axis Forces."

"The only way I could do that is to meet with Vargas. He's a dictator. Only his word could guarantee that."

"Exactly, and Admiral Canaris will go with you to minimize suspicions."

"Okay, but I've been seen by the guards who took me from my hotel and by Colonel Schneider. I'm a big guy. They'd be hard pressed to forget me."

"The men who took you to the Abwehr have already been sent to another town to investigate rumors of American activity. Schneider is not so easy. You'll have to find a way to avoid him, but you're going to the Presidential Palace, not the Abwehr."

"And, what do I use for proof? Is there a recording device?" She handed him a cigarette pack. "I'm not a smoker, and I'm sure you realize that. So, this must be the recorder."

"You will ask Vargas to sign a contract, attesting to his loyalty to the Reich. When he refuses, and he will, activate the recorder with the switch on the side of the pack."

"All right, but where are the cigarettes?"

"It isn't, oh yes, that's smart. There should be a couple of cigarettes in case someone sees the pack and asks for a smoke. We'll get some for you. You'll leave your hotel at six in the morning. Walk downhill to the laundry on the corner. It belongs to us. There you will change into your uniform, and the Admiral's car will pick you up in front of the building across the street. Do you understand?"

"Yes, but I do have one question. How did you first establish contact with Admiral Canaris?"

She grinned. "In bed."

Chapter Five

The streets were nearly empty when Berg walked down the sidewalk to the laundry, and there was little more traffic when he emerged, wrapped in black with the stunning SS insignia on his arm. He'd been careful to shave closely and to carry himself with the stiff, uncompromising air of a Nazi officer. His belt carried no Luger, but then it wouldn't befit an envoy sent on a peaceful mission. The pistol Lydia gave him was tucked away in his pants' pocket. By the time he reached the other side of the street, the staff car was already arriving. He climbed into the back seat only to see an unexpected face, Canaris, with pistol in hand.

"You may sit down facing me, Mr. Berg, if that is your real name. And, make no sudden moves."

"I'd be a foolish man not to listen with a Luger pointed at me." He nodded. "Well, Admiral, it looks like you have discovered me."

"You will sit quietly, not a word." He raised his voice. "Colonel Schneider, take us to the villa I told you about."

"You have a colonel driving you around? That's impressive."

"Matters of this importance must be entrusted only to the most reliable officers. You are dressed in a German uniform. I could shoot you now as a spy, but we have other plans first. You will say no more until I tell you to speak." They drove out of town, to a dirt road, and up a hill. As they passed through the iron gates, Canaris said, "This is the garden, Colonel. We have information that Mr. Berg has been meeting a British agent here. We will catch them together and be rid of both. Park the car behind those trees, out of sight."

The scent of fresh flowers caught his nose as Moe walked toward the rendezvous spot, Schneider's pistol in his back. "This place is actually quite beautiful in the daylight."

"Quiet!" Canaris barked. "If you know what's good for you, you will keep your mouth closed. Colonel, I suggest you search him."

Schneider rumbled through Moe's pockets and came out with the revolver. "Ah, look what we have."

"Give it to me." Canaris palmed the pistol and slipped his finger onto the trigger. "So, you have come here to do murder. Do you know what we do to men who offer us harm?"

"I'll bet it's not good."

"You will not be so smug when I am finished, Mr. Berg." He raised the gun and shot Schneider three times. "There, he will not be a problem any longer. I needed your pistol. It could be difficult to explain how he was shot with my gun, once his body is found."

"You don't fool around, do you, Admiral?" He knelt by the body, checked for a pulse, and rose again. "Well, he's dead enough. But, let's take a minute to think this thing through. We've got a German officer, shot to death. Somebody's going to investigate the hell out of this. Maybe we can do something to divert attention, once the colonel's body is found."

"If you have an idea that would be of help to me, I am listening."

"Tell me where he lived, and I'll plant something in his house to lead the investigators somewhere other than your office."

"Yes, I can see where your mind is going, perhaps drugs or something else that could show he traveled in dangerous company. But, how would you come by such items? You are but a short time in the country."

"I had the opportunity to make the acquaintance of a local woman yesterday, a lady in the relaxation business, and I believe she could help me with that."

"Very well, I can tell you how to get to his house as we drive to the President's Palace, but I must warn you, it is guarded. Even if you should slip by the guards, the house is securely locked. There will be no open windows to crawl through."

"I expected as much, and I have a plan for that as well."

"Of course, if you are caught, I would have no choice but to have you shot."

"Of course."

"Then we understand each other. Now, come, and I will drive us to the Presidential Palace."

"Are you going to leave his body there?"

"Not I. His killer left him there." He grinned and said, "Schneider was getting too close to uncovering my relationship with the Allies. He had to be eliminated before that happened. I will recommend him for a medal, posthumously of course. It will make his family proud. Such is the way of war."

Moe pushed out a long, exaggerated breath. "That sounds like the Third Reich is at war with itself, sort of like Congress."

* * * *

Berg had never seen as many armed guards in one building. He wondered how they'd get access to Vargas and, if they did, could they get out? Canaris checked his gun belt at the desk outside the presidential office. He clicked his heels and led Berg inside to opulent furnishings and to a smallish man seated with legs crossed. "Mr. President, may I introduce Captain Heinrich Berger."

"Good morning, Captain. Please be seated and tell me how I may be of service to you and the High Command."

"Thank you, your Excellency, and forgive my Portuguese. It is not my strongest language."

"I understand you perfectly well."

Moe pulled the recorder from his pocket. "May I offer you a cigarette?"

"No, thank you. I smoke only cigars."

He lowered the recorder into his lap and switched it on. "Then I will dispense with formalities and come to our business. The Fuhrer values his friendship with you and with Brazil, and I think you have seen his support of your regime in recent years."

"Yes, and I also value our friendship."

"I come on a sensitive matter, Mr. President. Some unfortunate rumors have found their way into the halls of the High Command that say you have pledged your support to America, should that country enter the war in Europe."

Vargas sat quietly for a moment, a thin smile creasing his face. "These are simply matters of diplomacy. I want no trouble from the United States, but I want Hitler to know I am his friend. Have we not opened our doors to your soldiers?"

"Of course you have, but you also have American bases." Berg drew a long, folded document from his jacket. "Would you agree to sign this statement, affirming your friendship and loyalty to the Third Reich?"

Canaris rapped his fist on the arm of his chair. "You must not ask that of the President. It is insulting and below the dignity of the High Command."

"But, I am under orders."

"Then I am revoking those orders, Captain, and you may tell your superiors that. If His Excellency gives us his word, then that is sufficient. He need not sign your statement or anything like it."

"Thank you, Admiral, and please don't be too harsh with the captain. Of course, you have my word, and I hope you will tell the Fuhrer himself that he can depend on Brazil."

Canaris stood and motioned for Berg to stand. "Then we will leave you. And, our most sincere thanks for your time." They slowly left the office, Canaris collected his gun belt, and they marched down the hallway. "Did you get your recording?"

"I did, Admiral."

"Then, let's get you out of the country before you find yourself in the hangman's noose."

* * * *

A long taxi ride and a short walk brought Berg to a clump of shrubs at the edge of a well-manicured lawn nearly hidden in the night. He sank to a spot between two large bushes bedazzled with red and yellow flowers and watched the guards patrol the grounds. An hour became two, and two became three, until it was nearly two o'clock, and Moe was satisfied that he understood their patterns. Two soldiers paced around the perimeter, walking by the front of the house once every thirty minutes with true German precision, and they always spoke to each other and to the soldier stationed at the door, as they passed. *That's perfect*, he thought. *And, my friends back home gave me something just right for you guys*. He took a pack of cigarettes from his coat pocket, pulled one of them out, and felt it to be sure the tiny capsule was still embedded in the tobacco. *Okay, boys, come and get them*. He tossed the pack into the path the soldiers followed so carefully, to a spot near a security light. The night sat deadly quiet, as he waited. *Where are you, boys? Come on, come on.* The first soldier reached the pack and passed it by. *Damn, pay attention.*

As he met the other soldier, they spoke, and the second soldier said, "What is that?" They stepped to the spot of light together. "Did you drop your cigarettes?"

"No, I ran out an hour ago." He knelt and picked the pack up. "It is nearly full. How did we miss this?"

The soldier at the door called to them. "What is happening there?"

"Cigarettes."

"Wait there. I want one." He joined the other two, popped a cigarette between his lips, and fired all three smokes with his lighter. "All right, let's smoke these and get back to work before the colonel comes home and finds us standing around." He was yet to make it back to the door when all three soldiers dropped to the ground.

"Well, Stanley, you make a nice Mickey Finn. Very effective." Berg rose and crossed the lawn, watching carefully for any sign of movement from the guards. He didn't need to crawl through an open window. He lifted the keys from the guard's belt, unlocked the house, and let himself in. But, he wasn't there to plant drugs. He was there to spy, and he was thrilled about it. The ornate foyer opened to a library, lined with books and works of art. Moe found a bottle of wine, poured himself a glass, and strolled about the house like he owned it. "Okay, Morris, get busy. Those guys won't stay knocked out forever." Most of the house left him pale, finding nothing of importance. And, then he found a locked briefcase stuffed behind the bed. "Well, well, what do we have here?" He took a paper clip from the dresser, sat on the edge of the bed, and worked the lock open. He thumbed through the pages until he found the one that spoke most loudly to him. "Hmm, a letter from Himler. You were running with some big shots in the Reich, Colonel Schneider. What does Heir Himler have to say? Oh, shit. They can't do that."

* * * *

Berg landed in New York and had but one night with Stella before leaving for Washington. He filed his report and then received a memo to meet John Clark in Q Building. The brief directions took him down a bustling hallway, up a flight of stairs in the back of the building, and to a set of offices with no identification on the doors. "Is this it?"

He walked in and was greeted by an aging receptionist. "Good morning. Are you Mr. Berg?"

"Yes. I have an appointment with, well, I suppose it's with Mr. Clark."

"May I see your credentials?' She looked them over carefully and then looked him over carefully. "Third door on the left."

The stale odor of burned tobacco permeated the hall, and every person he passed watched him go by. When he stepped into the office, a haze of smoke floated over three men, seated around a wide desk. Clark pointed to a chair. "Come in, Moe. I want you to meet some people." They shook Berg's hand, as Clark introduced them. "You know Woodrow Treadwell."

"I didn't know his name was Woodrow."

"And this is Bill Donovan, better known as Wild Bill, the head of OSS."

"Is that where we are, OSS?"

Donovan answered. "You are in the Office of Strategic Services, America's version of MI6. When John saw your report, he thought it well to share it with us. We've read the report and listened to your recording. Tell me, Mr. Berg, do you have anything more than this?"

"I believe I put everything in the report. Clearly, President Vargas has aligned himself with Hitler. As for what progress the Germans are making on an atomic bomb, I have only what Canaris and the girl told me."

"When you tie the two stories together, it gets alarming, but that's the problem. It's a story. Now, don't get me wrong, Moe. You brought us what could be a very damaging recording of a dictator I've never trusted, but it is only that, a recording. That could be anybody's voice. Even if it is Vargas, which I don't doubt, he could just be telling the Germans what they want to hear. If America should enter the war, and I'm not suggesting we will, then Brazil may well come running right back to us. There is an advantage to knowing the people you deal with, and we know Vargas."

"I'm sure you'd know better about that than I would, but what about the atomic research? They have access to uranium now, the kind needed for fission. We can't ignore that."

"That is the most troubling part. I spoke with President Roosevelt this morning and, by the way, he said to thank you for your work."

"Please tell him it was my pleasure."

"Don't get too carried away with a message from the President. He does that a lot." Donovan lit a cigarette. "Moe, are you sure they said Heisenberg is involved with the bomb project, Werner Heisenberg?"

"That's what they said."

"Well, that's a problem. Hahn is an idea guy, but with Heisenberg they've got a brilliant physicist who could actually run the project, make things happen. For now, there isn't much we can do. The President isn't going to drag the country into an expensive and bloody war without provocation, but he knows the time is coming. Say, do you still have the film you shot of Tokyo?"

"Yes, I have it stored in a safe place."

"Hold onto that. It may be needed, if we go to war. And, when we do, we're going to need people behind their lines in Germany and Japan and probably Italy. The United States has little experience with espionage, but we're learning, even with Hoover and his FBI trying to close this office down. But, that's another matter." He stood and faced the window. "You are one of the few Americans who have actually worked undercover in a foreign country. I've talked this over with Mr. Rockefeller, and we'd like to see you transfer into OSS."

"Okay."

Donovan wheeled around. "Just like that? No questions? No special requests? You didn't even know we existed until a few minutes ago."

"MI6 knows about you. I had dinner with their agent in Rio before I left. And, I would need the same accommodations I've had with Mr. Clark, free reign to do what needs to be done and ready access to money for bribes and equipment."

"Well, you won't need those things just yet. I can't get that kind of funding until we actually enter the war. There is a rigid training program, and then we'll assign you to something like the Balkans' desk. Through teletype and occasional trips, you should be able to keep in touch with what's going on in Europe. But, first we have to teach you what it really means to spy for your country, and we'll start that next week. When the time is right, we'll send you inside. It's a serious commitment, Moe. You could die doing this. Is there anything that would hold you back?"

He thought of Stella and how, even now, his heart yearned for her. "No, sir. Nothing will interfere with my work."

"Good, then we'll process the paperwork. Is there anything else, Berg?"

"You didn't mention the letter from Himler. It was in my report."

"Why didn't you bring it with you?"

"Because, I was afraid someone would look for it after they found Schneider's body and, if it were missing, they'd know something was up with his murder. But, the message was clear. Himler wanted Schneider to join the project to kidnap Pope Pius to retaliate for Mussolini's arrest."

"Listen to me, Moe. You've come back with a couple of pretty tall tales, atomic super weapons and a plot against the leader of the Catholic Church. They sound a bit fantastic, like the kind of stories a man invents to make himself look more important. It's not that I don't believe you, but I need something more than your word, if I'm to go to President Roosevelt with this."

"Look, Hitler tried to destroy the church in Germany, because it was a threat to his absolute authority, and you know how Pope Pius spoke out when Germany invaded Poland. I know it sounds like a crazy plot, but we're dealing with a crazy man."

"Vatican City is a country unto itself. Invading Italy doesn't mean they would invade the Vatican. There's a difference."

"Come on, Bill. The Vatican is guarded by a bunch of guys wearing tights and carrying spears. They couldn't protect my ass." Berg walked to the door and turned back. "Wait a minute. If they wanted to take the Pope, they could've already done it. He's not at the Vatican, is he?"

"What makes you say that? The man lives there. It's his home, his castle. Where would he be, but the Vatican?"

"Not London, too many bombing raids. And, not France either. He'd be hard to hide in America. Yeah, somewhere neutral, somewhere he feels safe."

"That's enough, Moe. Let's not talk about this anymore."

"Can you keep him out of Rome for the rest of the war?"

"We can't keep him out of anywhere. The man's the pope. He goes where he wants to go."

"Then, in time, he'll go back to Rome, and Hitler will kill him. We've got to do something about this."

"I hear what you're saying, Moe, and I'll take it all under advisement."

"Take it under advisement? Well, I may need to do more than that."

* * * *

Evening settled on the waters of the Atlantic with Moe and Stella stretched over a sofa on a hotel-room balcony, wrapped in each other's arms. She slipped her hand inside his sweater, dragging a fingernail down his bare chest, and the warmth from the wine brought a smile to his face. "Your chest is a smooth as mine, Moe."

"Oh? Shall we compare to see whether that's true?"

"You're a bad boy, but give me another glass of wine, and I might consider it." She held up her flute as he filled it, and then took a sip before setting it on the floor. "Did you ask whether the OSS could station you in New York?"

"They don't have an office here yet."

"Then you could be the guy who opens one for them. I miss you when you're gone."

"I know, Stella, me too. But, we're on the cusp of war, and I can't stand idly and watch that mad man march to our front door. Sooner or later a German u-boat will sink one of our commercial ships and, like the Great War, whether we want it or not, we'll be in the middle of it. And, if they're going to send me to places like the Balkans, I might as well leave from Washington as from here."

"The Balkans is a long way."

"Not as far as Japan or Russia. We can be thankful for that, and I shouldn't be gone more than a few weeks at a time."

"That reminds me. Did you see the letter from Japan?"

"Yes, it's from my friend Eiji Sawamura, the young pitcher I met on my last trip there. He was only seventeen when I met him, but what a talent. We've been writing each other, on occasion, for several years. He says the Emperor is cracking down on communications between Japanese citizens and anyone is the US, and this would probably be his last letter."

"Oh, that's sad."

"Yeah, he seemed like a good kid. It's not his fault that they taught him to hate America. He's going to enlist in the Imperial Army soon. I hope he doesn't get himself killed."

"I hope you don't get yourself killed either, Moe."

He stroked the side of her face and said, "Why in the world would you think I might get killed?"

"I'm no fool. Costa Rica was okay, but I know what kinds of things are going on in Brazil. The Nazis are swarming down there, and you walked right into the middle of it. And, when you got back, you joined some secret department that wants to train you how to spy. They don't train you unless they plan to use you, Moe. You're right. We'll be in the war before long, and they're going to ship you some place like Germany or Italy and leave me here to cry myself to sleep every night. They shoot spies, you know."

She was right, and he knew it. But, how could he ever admit it, to her or to himself? He pulled himself up, scooped her thin body into his arms, and set her on the railing. "I would throw myself down off this balcony before I'd hurt you, but there are some things I must do. If I have to go, I'll do my best not to get shot."

"Don't tease me. Promise me. Swear to me that you won't let them kill you and break my heart."

"What can I say to that?" He kissed her warmly and then looked into her eyes. "Marry me, Stella. We'll go to the courthouse tomorrow, and then I'll have to come back to you."

"I would marry you in a minute, but I know you too well. The truth is that you are going to leave me. It's in your blood. This idea of risking your life for your country has infected you. It's like a fever, and I can't fix it."

"No, no, it's not like that."

"It is exactly like that. I'll wait for you, I'll worry about you, and I'll relish the days we have, but I'll not marry you until you're free of this virus." The ringing of the telephone drew her from the rail and into the room. Moe stood staring at the ocean, trying to deny what he knew was true. Then she stepped back outside. "Moe, that was Ethel. There was a radio broadcast. The Japanese have bombed Pearl Harbor."

* * * *

Speculation was over, America joined the war, and Moe Berg found himself on an estate in the Catoctin Mountains of Maryland. He raised an automatic pistol, resting the hilt in the palm of his left hand, to shoot at a target of Hitler, but his instructor stopped him. "Why are you holding your weapon that way?"

"Oh, Mr. Treadwell, I didn't see you. Uh, I'm trying to steady the weapon for a better shot."

"Do you think the Nazis will give you time to steady your weapon before blowing your head off? The answer is no, Mr. Berg. We don't go target shooting behind enemy lines. You must learn to shoot with one hand and do it efficiently."

"Very well." He fired six times and lowered the gun. "There, all solid hits to the chest."

"Why didn't you shoot the head?"

"Because, it's easier to miss when you aim at the head."

"You will not miss. You can't afford to. By the time you leave this camp, you will shoot quickly and accurately, and you will shoot to kill." He raised his voice to the other eleven men at the range. "Agent Berg has just learned a valuable lesson. See to it that you all learn. A shot to the chest might kill a man. A shot to the head puts him down. Now, secure your weapons and move into the next room." Each trainee removed the clip from his gun, ejected the bullet in the chamber, and holstered his weapon. They stepped into an open room, and Treadwell said, "Today we will work on two techniques you may find of value in defending yourselves." He motioned for two trainees to face each other. "Agent Harding will play the part of an unarmed suspect, and Agent Wilson will draw his pistol, as if he were arresting him. Go ahead, gentlemen."

Wilson reached for his holster, and Harding dove at him, grabbing his arm with both hands. They grappled about the room, bumping into other trainees, until the gun came out and Wilson clicked the trigger twice, and

92

Treadwell stepped in. "All right, that's enough. Agent Harding, do you see a problem with the approach you took."

"Well, yeah, I guess. I mean he simulated getting off two shots. Even if the bullets hadn't hit me, the noise would've drawn attention to us. But, it's the best I could do, given the circumstances."

"It is not the best you can do, not if you are to be an OSS agent. Re-holster your weapon, Agent Wilson, and draw it again slowly." As he drew the gun from the holster, Treadwell took his hand and pulled it straight up. "There, you see. Let the force of his arm coming upward work with you. Then step in, twist his arm around yours, preferably your shoulder, and take him to the ground. Once you have leverage, wrap your fingers around the hammer, so he can't get off a shot. When you have him down with the hammer secured, then you can put you shin across his neck and bite his fingers until he releases the gun. Of course, if you have a knife, it's easier to simply slit his throat."

"In cold blood?"

"Just as cold as you can make it, Agent Harding. We are at war. The enemy will kill you without a second thought. If you are captured, they will torture you and then kill you. Expect no mercy from the Nazis and extend none to them."

"Yes, sir, but the hammer on a Luger is concealed in the weapon."

"Unfortunately, the Luger presents that problem for us, and it is the pistol of choice by the German military. Try not to get yourself arrested by one of those gentlemen. Now, I have one more technique to show you, and then you can practice what you've learned. Agent Berg, please step in front of me."

"All right. I've been kind of waiting for this."

"Yes, we'll see. How tall are you, Agent?"

"Six-three."

"I estimate your weight at two-hundred-twenty pounds. I stand five-feet-seven-inches tall and weigh one-hundred-fifty-five pounds. One would expect Agent Berg to pound me into dust with little effort." He took three steps back. "Please have at me, and give it your best effort."

"Okay, but remember you asked for it." As Berg stepped forward, Treadwell dropped to a crouch and kicked his knee from under him. The little man swung around his back and struck him at the base of his neck, and all four of Berg's limbs went numb. He fell with a thud, tingling and wondering what happened. Treadwell massaged his neck for a moment and then helped him to his feet. "What in the hell did you do to me?"

"I made use of a chuto strike. Agent Berg, would you please drop to one knee?'

"Only if you promise not to hit me again."

"Gentlemen, you will note this area of the spinal column. It is called the brachial plexus, a collection of nerves. The chuto strike uses the side of the palm, here, the heel, and the angle is thus. Do you see that?" They all muttered and nodded. "Properly applied, you can disable the largest of opponents. Improperly applied, you can break his neck or, worse yet, not disable him at all, and then he kills you." They spent the next hour disarming and disabling each other before moving on to the art of silent killing. And, so went the next three weeks.

The days were filled with training courses and workouts. They ran, shot, and fought, but they also learned to crack a safe by touch alone. They practiced deciphering codes, sending messages by Morse Code, and holding their breath for the three minutes it took to swim through a pipe. Berg was in better shape than he'd been since working at a lumber camp ten years before. When he wasn't in psychological evaluations, he read about the principles of fission in physics books and, on rare occasions, he wrote to Stella.

My Dearest Stella,

I have but a few minutes to write you. I am well, as I pray you are. We have long workdays here, but they are exhilarating. I wish I could tell you all I've seen and learned, but that I cannot do. I don't know what it is about the brisk air, or maybe it's the robust exercise, but I feel more alive than I have in years. There is something very natural about this work, but I miss you terribly. It was that way with baseball. I loved it, and yet it often denied us time together. And, for that, I hated it.

My superiors are tight-lipped about when we'll complete our training, but I hope to return to Washington before spring. Then I shall come to see you, even if I have to go AWOL to do it. Till then, please keep my side of the bed warm. All my love (every ounce),

Moe

On the fourth week, Treadwell called for Berg in his room. They left the main house and crossed the open lawns to a long, narrow building covered by the shade of oak trees. "Moe, you will be working with the men in this building soon, and you need to meet them."

"That's the first time you've called me Moe since we've been here."

"And, I'd appreciate your not sharing that with the other trainees. Some of them won't complete the training, and the ones that do will likely die in a foreign land. It isn't prudent for someone like me to form friendships with the agents only to see them fall."

"Then, why me? Am I the only one coming to this building?"

"For now you are. As to why I handle you differently, it's because your mission is different, and I will be your contact while you're on it. There's a reason why you are the only one studying physics. That will become clear to you soon, if it hasn't already." Treadwell unlocked the door, and they stepped inside. A hallway centered the building with rooms set to each side. They turned into the first room on the right. "Agent Berg, this is Stanley Lovell. He works on special technologies and weaponry."

"May I call you Stan?"

"Sure, most everybody does. Woody told me he was bringing you, so let's get right to it. Here are a couple of things we're developing. When you look at this table, what do you see?"

"I see a plate of oysters, probably steamed, and a stack of pancakes. Is this a dinner meeting?"

"You don't want this dinner, I assure you. Each of these items is prepared with an explosive compound. Here you have something as common as pancakes, which can be used to quickly eliminate an enemy."

"Do they give indigestion?"

"Well, I don't know. They're not intended for consumption."

"And, if I find myself in a restaurant and some Gestapo officer thinks it odd that I'd be eating flapjacks in Germany, he may put a Luger to my head and challenge me to eat them. I'd like to know whether your explosives will blow my guts out."

Treadwell motioned toward the door. "I'm sure Stan will work that out. Come on, I want you to see our forgery area."

They walked toward the far end of the hall, and Moe said, "I noticed he called you Woody. Is that what they call you in here?"

"Only in here. Anywhere else I am Mr. Treadwell or Agent Treadwell."

"Woody? I like that. Does it come from Woody Woodpecker?"

"You're a funny one. I hope that sense of humor doesn't get you killed one day. Okay, step in here."

"Whoa, hold on a minute. What about the guy back there, the one smoking and drinking beer? Is that Lucky Luciano? I've seen his picture in the papers. Why would you have someone from Murder Incorporated working here?"

"Mr. Luciano's past offenses are well documented, and he received the proper prison sentence for them. He has contacts in Italy, contacts who can help us. In exchange for his assistance, we had him brought here from prison. He helps us, and we help him."

"And, the men who forge documents, are they criminals too?"

"Do you know anyone better at forgery than those who made their living doing it? No, I thought not. These men have sorted pasts, but they're working for their country now. We need them. Does that satisfy your curiosity, Agent Berg?"

"It does, and I wasn't judging, only trying to understand."

"Good, then let's step inside." The door opened to a curly-haired man seated at a table, staring into a magnifying glass. "This is Morgan. He will provide you with identification papers under a variety of names and for a variety of countries."

Berg stepped forward and offered his hand. "Hello, Morgan. I'm glad to meet you." Morgan answered with a grunt. "Say, that binder, is that your book of credentials?"

"Yeah, I've got copies of identification papers for damn-near every government agency there is, including Europe, all in alphabetical order." He stroked the binder and said, "This is my baby. They took her from me when I got arrested, but now she's back, and she ain't never leaving me again."

"You have a right to be proud of your work. Do you mind if I take a look?"

"I reckon it's all right, so long as your hands are clean."

Berg opened the binder and flipped back to the F tab. "I'd like for you to make me credentials for this group."

"Why in the hell would you want that?"

"I have a feeling that I may need it one day, maybe soon." Morgan grunted again, and Berg turned for the door. "Shall we go, Mr. Treadwell?"

"What did you ask him for?"

Moe put a finger to his lips. "It's classified."

* * * *

A dozen men sat around a long, wooden table, dining on steak and lobster, served on china and complimented with bottles of Cabernet Sauvignon. Agent Harding sat next to Berg, his blond hair slicked back, and a striped bowtie cinched around his neck. "They feed us well here, don't they, Moe?"

"Like a man getting his last meal on death row."

"Uh, yeah, that's not what I meant. I'm just saying I could get used to eating like this. We haven't seen much steak in Missouri since the stock market fell in '29. Roosevelt's New Deal didn't do much for our people."

"I'm sad to here that, Bobby. It is Bobby, isn't it?"

"That's right, Robert Alexander Harding, named for my grandfather. I was the first one in my family to go to college." He shoved a slice of meat into his mouth and said, "I guess we've had little time to get to know each other, any of us, with all the training. We heard a little about you from the newspapers. The last I heard you were catching for the Red Sox." Berg didn't answer. "You are a quiet one, aren't you? Some of us guys come down here at night to have a beer or two together, but not you. You're always off somewhere, by yourself. So, tell me, Moe, who are you? Where are you from? Do you have a wife, a girlfriend?"

"I am Morris Berg, the catcher for the Red Sox." Then he started to lie. "And, no, I have no wife or girlfriend. My father was a sharecropper in the Deep South before moving to Kansas. He had a hardware store out there until he died of cancer two years ago. My mother was killed in a car wreck a year later. So, there's no one but me. Just solitary old Morris Berg, wondering whether he can cut the mustard with the OSS."

"I wonder when they'll tell us our assignments. Have they told you yet?"

Moe looked down the table, leaned closer, and whispered, "Don't let this get around, but they suspect the Nazis could be trying to take control of the subway in New York. I'm going to spend my days moving from one train to another, looking for suspicious characters. It's perfect for me, because I love riding the subway."

"That sounds absolutely dreadful. In fact, I think it might be bull shit."

"And, I think you might be a German spy, a double agent."

"That's crazy, Moe. I'm from Missouri for heaven's sake. Look at me, I'm, okay, I get it. Now, I understand why no one has befriended you. You are an ass hole."

"That I am, Bobby. That I am."

* * * *

Dinner ended, and Berg retired to his room to read an article penned by Werner Heisenberg's on his Uncertainty Theory. A rap came from the door. "Come in."

Treadwell stepped in, closed the door, and opened a manila folder. "I have your training challenge. Each of the trainees will be given a government complex of some kind with instructions to retrieve sensitive information from it, by hook or by crook. The one difference between this exercise and a field assignment is that we don't kill our own people. So, if you're caught, escape if you can, but don't shoot anybody."

"I'll try to control my savage nature. Where do I go?"

"The Glenn Martin aircraft factory in Baltimore. In this folder, we have your identification and a letter of introduction on White House stationary, both forged of course."

"Courtesy of our Mr. Morgan I take it."

"Yes, and he included the credentials you asked him to make. I won't ask you about those, as I do not wish to know. Glenn Martin is working on a new design, the B-26 Marauder, and you are to bring back copies of the blueprints for the engine design." He handed the folder to Berg.

"So, I'm a quality inspector for the Air Force. That should get me into some privileged areas, but I'll be escorted. Getting pictures of the prints won't be easy."

"Staying alive behind enemy lines isn't easy either." He pulled a military cap from behind his back and set it on the bed. "This should help you with the pictures."

"A present from Stan?"

"A mini camera is sewn into the lining on the front of the cap. Take a look at it."

Berg rolled the cap in his hands and said, "Is this the switch in the sweatband?"

"Very good, Moe. You won't be able to take pictures of all the blue prints. We're looking for something that shows the particulars of the new engines. You insist on seeing the prints to compare those specifications to what you see on the shop floor. Snap a couple of photos and you're home free. It's just that simple."

"You sound very confident."

"And, you're not?"

"Oh, I'll get the pictures. The question is whether I can get them without going to prison."

Chapter Six

The insignia of an Air Force major rode on the shoulders of his uniform, and Moe Berg stepped out of the taxi and adjusted the sleeves of his jacket. His forged credentials gained him passage through the gate at the Glenn Martin factory, but that was just the beginning of his mission. A set of glass doors swung open, and a man dressed in white shirt, gray tie, and navy pants stepped out to greet him. "Good morning, Major Haddock. I'm Peter Jansen, plant manager for this facility."

Berg towered over the be-speckled, middle-aged man. "And, good morning to you, Mr. Jansen. Shall we get down to business?"

"Well, I thought you might like a cup of coffee first."

"Coffee can wait. Here is my letter of authorization." Jansen scanned the letter, ran a finger over the White House header, and nodded. "I'd like to see the design documents, and then I want to see your manufacturing process. "

"Yes, of course." He handed the letter back to Berg and gestured for him to come in. They passed through a paneled lobby, between two rows of desks with typewriters clicking, and out the back door into the factory. "If you don't mind, it might be easier to see the process first. We go right past it on the way to the Engineering Department."

"That's fine, but I don't need to see the entire process, just where you build the engines."

"Please be careful crossing the forklift aisle. Yes, that's fine, that's good. Now, Major, if you'll step right up there on the platform, you'll have a bird's-eye view of our assembly line."

Berg clanked down the metal runway, leaned over the rail, and grabbed the bill of his cap, as if to keep it from falling. "What are your tolerances when machining the parts?" He clicked a photo, as Jansen answered.

"All our parts are normalized at five thousandths of an inch. We find that using a standard tolerance makes it simpler to move employees from one area to another. We do it for efficiency."

"Then I should see that in the design documents. Let's go there now. I've seen enough here."

They descended back to the concrete floor and walked the two hundred feet to a plywood-enclosed office. Jansen didn't bother to introduce any of his engineers, but went straight to a drawing board. "When the security guard told me why you were here, I had my people put these prints out for you." He splayed his fingers over the long schematic to hold it flat and said, "As you can see, this is a cross-sectional view of the engine. We can generate more horsepower on less fuel than conventional engines, and that makes for longer bombing runs with heavier payloads. Here, please, step closer and look for yourself."

Berg slipped his cap off, held it in the crook of his arm, and started clicking pictures. The tiny thumbwheel made it awkward for him to advance the film after each shot, but he managed to take three pictures before he felt cold steel on the back of his neck. "Tell me if I'm wrong, Mr. Jansen, but that feels very much like the barrel of a gun."

"You are exactly right, Major, and if you so much as flinch, my security man will be forced to blow your head off. Now, you march yourself into that back office and stand against the wall." Berg put his hands behind his head and walked quietly into the room. "Keep your gun on him, George, while I call my contacts."

"Before you do that, could I show you something?"

"I'm not sure you have anything I want to see."

"Please. You see, I'm in training, and I was sent here as a test of my preparedness. It appears I have failed miserably; although, I'm not sure how you discovered me."

Jansen set the telephone receiver back down. "My first clue was that you came in a cab. Majors have drivers. Their egos would not allow anything less, but you're from out of town, so I thought the taxi could be legitimate. Then I tested you by saying all our tolerances are the same. Every government inspector we've had has been an engineer, and any decent engineer would know that some parts require tighter tolerances than others. And, the last straw was the way you reacted to having a gun put to your head. Majors in every army in the world have a certain arrogance. They think they're generals in the making, and they behave like that. If you were a real major, you would've chewed my ass out for that, but you didn't. Overall, you were just too courteous."

"Everything you have said is true, and I am sorely embarrassed. May I show you my identification? It's in my shoe."

Jansen sat on the edge of the desk. "All right, let's see it, but don't forget about that gun. Given a reason, he will kill you."

"And, I don't intend to give him a reason." Berg bent down, eased off his shoe, and pulled the heel open. He handed a small, leather pouch to Jansen.

"So, your name is Harvey Candler?"

"No, sir, it's Harold Chandler. I'm afraid it's a name Mr. Hoover won't forget when I get back to the office."

"That's your problem. We've been on good terms with the FBI, but we won't be, if I let one of his trainees get away with posing as a government official." He reached for the receiver again. "You stand right where you are, and I'll get your people on the phone."

Berg knelt and put his shoe back on. As he rose, he grabbed the guard's wrist, took his arm up, and twisted it behind him. A sharp chop to the brachial plexus, at exactly the right angle, and the guard fell, his gun now in Berg's hand. "Put the phone down. I'm sure you'll make your call after I'm gone, but I'd rather face Mr. Hoover without being in handcuffs. I'm sorry about this, but I have to go. My apologies to your guard." He opened the cylinder and let the bullets fall from the revolver, smashed the window with a chair, and scampered out.

His mind raced, as he tried to find a way out without getting shot. *Okay, Morris, now what? You have no taxi, and you don't drive. Well, don't just stand there.* He sprinted down the side of the building and cut through a narrow alley. Sirens wailed as he stopped at the end of the alley, looking for somewhere, anywhere, to hide. His gaze fell on a row of Marauders in the post-production staging area, and he made a mad dash for the nearest one. But, before he could get there, a guard ran up to him, pistol drawn. Berg skidded to a stop, remembered what Jansen had told him, and he barked at the guard. "Holster that weapon before it goes off and go secure the front gate. Tell them to be on the lookout for a squatty man in a light-blue jacket. Do you understand?"

"Yes, sir, Major."

"Then what are you waiting for? Go." The man scampered away, and Berg slowed to a walk. He paced by a Quonset hut, checked to see whether anyone was watching, and slipped under the wing of the first bomber. *Okay, you're here. Now, where do you hide? Ah, that looks interesting.* He pulled himself up through the open bomb bay doors and cranked them shut with the emergency closing device. *Thank you for not changing this part of the design, Mr. Jansen. I might be toast without it.* And, he settled in for a long wait. The afternoon sun beat against the metal fuselage, and sweat soaked his borrowed uniform, all to the sound of the footsteps and voices of the men searching for him.

Evening covered the factory grounds in darkness, save for a few light posts that shone through the plane's windshield. Still Berg waited, but he knew he had to get out before dawn. When his watch swept past two o'clock, it was time to go. He patiently lowered the bomb bay doors and dropped to the ground. *Maybe they're not looking for me anymore. Maybe they think I escaped. And, maybe not.* He made a break for the back fence, but he stopped as he crossed the road. The stop sign, yes. He yanked on it, pulling from side to side, until it came loose. When he reached the fence, he used the sign like a crude shovel to break dirt loose and dragged clods out with his hands. It felt like digging his own grave. *Hurry, man, you know they patrol these fences.* Finally he cleared enough space to crawl under the fence, at the expense of a few buttons off his jacket. "Thank, God," he whispered. "Now get back to camp and see whether you're going to prison."

* * * *

The remainder of the night and most of the next day passed before Berg found his way back to the Catoctin Mountains. He went to his room and showered without a word to anyone. But, he was not to hide for long. A knock came at his door. "Moe, are you in there?"

He slid off the bed and opened the door. "Agent Treadwell, I didn't expect to see you till morning."

Treadwell stepped in and closed the door. "Sit down, Berg. We need to talk."

Moe sank onto the foot of the bed. "I guess you heard about what happened."

"J. Edgar is mad as hell, calling everybody in the intelligence community, accusing each one of giving him the blame for a botched mission."

"Does he know it was me?"

"You? Why would he think that?" Treadwell propped his foot on the bed. "Anytime you or any other agent is discovered, we will deny any knowledge of your existence and your mission. And, that's exactly what we did with Hoover. Now, did you get the pictures?"

"Yes. There in the cap on the dresser."

"Then your mission was a success."

"But, they found me out. If that were the Nazis, I'd be dead."

"Indeed, you would, but if you completed your mission, then your death, while unfortunate, would be an investment in freedom." Treadwell walked to the dresser and took the cap. "I have bad news for you, Moe."

"I was expecting that. Am I fired?"

"Your father died. Take three days, go home, and get back as soon as you can."

At first, Moe didn't know how to feel. His father had been a difficult man, a stern and uncompromising parent, who had treated Moe's one genuine love like a leper. And, then the pain cut through his chest, he trembled, and tears wet his face.

* * * *

Bernard Berg's body lay in a wooden casket, surrounded by white satin and dressed in his normal work clothes, including a freshly starched apron. His three children stood quietly, staring at his remains with the scent of not-so-fresh flowers in the air. Moe shoved his hands into his pockets and said, "I appreciate your arranging for me to see the body. I know it cuts against tradition." He rubbed the side of his face and groaned. "I guess that's it. I mean, what do you say when the man who raised you is gone?"

"You could tell him you love him."

"You would be the one to say that, Ethel, and I'm sure you mean it. But, somehow, it would sound so hollow. I don't know that I could do that. No, you tell him, Sam."

"Me? I didn't have to wait till he died to tell him that. We had a great relationship. You're the one who disappointed him, not me."

"Don't say that. Moe wasn't meant to be a doctor or teacher like us. He was a baseball player and a good one. And, now he's going to be a government employee of some kind. Papa would be proud of Moe." She smiled and said, "By the way, Moe, what is your job."

"I can't talk about it."

"You see, Ethel? Even now, with Papa dead, he can't settle down. He has some mysterious job nobody can know about. I don't buy it. You just can't grow up, can you, Moe? Papa was right. You'll never be responsible for anything, not even that girl out there in the parlor."

"Don't worry about that girl, Sam. You can say what you like about me, just like he did, but I'll kick your ass, if you say anything about Stella."

"I've got nothing against her, but anytime you want to try kicking my ass, come ahead. We can go outside and take care of that right now."

"Stop it, you two. Are you going to beat each other up with Papa laying there dead? Will you go to his funeral with torn clothes and bruises? You'd break Mama's heart. Think about her for a change, will you?"

"She's right, Sam. I can whip your ass some other time." He glanced at his watch. "It looks like time to go. We don't need to make him late for his own funeral."

Ethel snickered and then covered her mouth. "You are a bad man, Moe Berg. I can tell you didn't go to synagogue often enough."

"That's one thing Papa and I had in common. Neither of us was very good at being a practicing Jew."

Sam shrugged and said, "Papa respected tradition though. He may have opened his shop on the Sabbath, but he never missed reading the Torah or following the rest of the law. Regardless of what you might think, he loved his family."

Moe checked his watch again. "Well, children, let's go. We've got a long, tedious funeral to attend and seven days of mourning. We'd better get to it."

* * * *

The Star of David, his name, and the span of his life were the only carvings in Bernard Berg's simple tombstone. Moe stood between his mother and sister, as a light rain began. "It's not much to define a man's life, is it, Mama?"

"No. Your father was much more than we could've put on a marker, and he would've wanted it to be simple. That was his way, to work twelve hours a day and build a life for his family. I just didn't expect to lose him so soon."

"Yes, I know. So much left unsaid, so much unresolved, harsh words I can't take back."

"Don't punish yourself, son. Your father could be a hard man, who spoke his mind, but he loved you. You should never doubt that." She took his hand. "Come, let's go home. You'll feel better when you've had something to eat."

"You and Ethel go ahead. I need to talk with Stella, and we'll meet you at the house." They parted, and Moe crossed the cemetery, being careful not to step on the graves. He stepped into the passenger's side of the car, and Stella gave him a warm hug. "I needed that. I wish you had come with us."

She sat upright. "Your father would not have wanted me there."

"He would've gotten over that in time. Once he got to, well, maybe not. He could be a stubborn ass when he wanted to. I never thought I'd miss him this much."

"It's tough to lose a parent. I know. You have some tough days ahead, but you don't have to go through them alone."

"Mama wants us to come to the house and eat."

"Ah, that great American tradition, the grief buffet."

"I guess you could call it that. I think everyone she knows brought a casserole of some kind. What do you say? It'll give us some time with her before I have to go back to Washington."

"Does that mean you're finished with your training?"

"I'm finished in Maryland. They gave me three days funeral leave, and then I go to DC for my first assignment."

"What's it going to be?"

"I can't say. I know what you're going to say and, before you start, they told me I'd be stationed somewhere in Washington, at least for the foreseeable future. That won't be so bad, sort of like when I was in Boston and we commuted to see each other."

"Moe, Moe, Moe. You don't get it, do you? Yes, we had some great weekends when you were with the Red Sox, and there was something almost clandestine about the train ride, but it was only weekends. Now, you've been gone for weeks and, as soon as you get home, we're back to being part-time lovers."

"Come on, Stell. Surely, we can make this work until the war's over. I have a duty."

"Duty. That's all I hear these days. It's all over the radio. What about your duty to me?" She swiped her hand across the steering wheel and groaned. "I know, I know. I'm being selfish. The country's at war, and you're doing your part. Some women lose their men for years at a time. Some lose them forever. But, when you played ball, at least we could talk about your work. I could go to the games. Now, everything's a secret with you, Moe. I can't share that part of your life, and I feel a little deserted. I'm afraid I'll lose you all together."

"That's not going to happen." He stroked her dark hair. "Marry me, Stella Huni. We'll go right now and celebrate with a big helping from the grief buffet."

She paused, looked out over the cemetery, and turned to Moe. "I'm tempted to say yes, but I won't, not now. I'm not a government agent, but I can see where you're headed. Yes, you'll have an office in Washington for a while, and then they'll ship you off to war. Once you're over there for a year or two, you'll forget about me."

"Don't say that. I waited all my life for you."

"Then prove it, Moe. Go do your duty in Europe or Africa or wherever else they ship you. When you come home, if you still want me, I'll marry you then. But, tonight I'm going to make love to you like I have never done before."

"Yeah? Well, then, that being the case, maybe we should skip dinner. Mama will understand."

* * * *

Moe's father was buried, and his love for Stella was stronger than ever, but something still burned in his soul.

111

Something he'd put off too long. He folded his newspaper and laid it on the seat beside him. He turned to the plane's window and ran his gaze over snow-covered mountains, stretching in every direction. "Switzerland, how beautiful," he whispered. "Enjoy the view, while you can, Morris. You may be fired when you get home." For the first time, he was blatantly ignoring his bosses at the OSS, but he didn't care. When the plane landed, he knew it was too late to back out."

The Customs' guard barked at him. "Papers." Moe handed him his passport. "You are Australian?"

"I am."

"And, what business do you have in Switzerland, Mr. Robinson?"

"I am travelling for business."

"What is your business here?"

"I am an art dealer, here to consider an offering from one of your local artists. We hear she is very talented, and we may wish to display her work at our museum in Sydney." The guard stared at him, and Moe fought back the temptation to say more. *Don't do it. Make him ask what he wants to know.* The guard waved him through, and Moe hired a car and driver. They drove southwest from Bern, past Munsingen, to a narrow road near the village of Spiez. "Take me to the villa at the top of this mountain." He told the driver.

"But, no one goes to that villa."

"That will not be true today for I am going."

"As you wish, sir."

The long Mercedes struggled to maneuver the winding road but, in time, they reached an iron gate. Berg stepped out, only to be met by an armed guard. "Turn your automobile around and go back down the mountain."

"But, I wish to speak with the man of this house," Berg said.

The guard swung his rifle up and pressed the barrel into Moe's chest. "There is no one at this house. If you value your life, you will leave now."

"Very well, but let me compliment you on doing such a good job of protecting no one." He climbed back into the car, and they drove away. They rounded a second curve, and Berg said, "Pull over." The driver stopped the car, saying nothing, and Moe opened his door. "I'm going to stay here for a while. You drive to the village and come back for me in two hours."

"But, sir, it gets very cold on the mountains. I fear for your safety."

"I fear for my safety too, but don't let that concern you. Here, this should be more than enough money for your time, and I will pay you more once you return. Can I count on you?"

"You can, but you will not be able to get past the gates."

"I don't intend to. Just make sure you don't forget about me."

"I will be back, but I will not wait for long."

"That's fair enough." Berg stepped out and watched the car disappear. He didn't want to get shot and he didn't want to hurt a guard who had done him no harm, so he skirted the gate and took to the rocks. How would he make it across and then up the rugged cliff? He didn't know, but he was on his way. The first half hour was hard, and the second half hour worse. Scrub brush tore at his clothes, crags ripped his hands, and the blasts of wind tried to knock him off, as he pulled and slipped and climbed. And, at the top of the precipice, he found level ground and a rifle aimed at his head. "Good afternoon, good sir." The guard shifted his head to call for help, but Berg snatched the gun from his hands and turned it on him. "I don't want to hurt you, but take me to him and do it now." The man was unrelenting. "Damn it, man, I'm dead serious."

A mild voice spoke from behind him. "If you have come to kill me, I am here, son."

Berg turned to face a thin man dressed in papal gowns. "I am not here to kill you. I came to help you."

"Then we must have a cup of tea." Berg handed the rifle back to the guard and followed the Pope to a table overlooking the village and a grand lake. "Please sit, my son."

"With all due respect, sir, I am not your son. I'm Jewish."

"We are all God's children."

"I have a matter of great importance to discuss with you."

"That was apparent to me by the way you arrived. Please forgive me for refusing you at the gate, but these are dangerous times, and someone like me must take precautions." He poured two cups of hot tea from a silver flask. "Have some of this and relax. Then we will talk."

Hot and slightly sweet, it ran down Berg's throat like a potion, easing his tight muscles and his tortured mind. And, for a moment, things weren't as frantic. The war was far away, and he felt only the serenity of mountains that rose in shades of blue and purple and white. He set his cup on the table and said, "I can see why you come here, but this is fantasy."

"It is God's creation. Everything is His creation."

"That is true, but some of His creation has gone awry. Hitler is murdering people by the hundreds of thousands, probably millions. And, now he wants to come after you."

"Why would a man of his power want to harm a simple man of God?"

"Let's not play that. You are the head of an enormous church, and the Catholics in Germany listen to you. He can't have that. Men are plotting as we speak to take you prisoner as soon as you return to the Vatican."

"How do you know this to be true?"

"I work for an American intelligence agency and I saw the orders, signed by Heinrich Himmler himself. There is an SS general named Karl Wolff, who will coordinate your kidnapping and take you north. If you don't come out in support of Hitler, they'll kill you. Look, we're going to liberate Rome within a few months. The Fifth Army is marching on Italy right now. All you need to do is stay out of Rome until it's safe."

"It is much to think about, but my people need me. They cannot see their leader in hiding. Where is my faith if I am not willing to be the light I was called to be?"

"You don't believe me, do you? Okay, what if you heard it from a Nazi officer? Would you believe him?" The Pope drank his tea without answering. "Do this for me. Before you go back to Rome, visit Spain. I know a German admiral who is friendly with us, and he often has reason to be in Madrid. If he confirms what I said, will you wait?

"How would you arrange this meeting?"

"The admiral and I have a mutual acquaintance at MI6. I can't say more than that, not even to you."

"You have come here at great risk to yourself, and I must respect that, but you must understand that I cannot and will not shrink in fear to Hitler or anyone else. Such is not my calling. But, having said that, I will wait and I will meet with your admiral."

"Thank you. May I use your telephone to make the call?"

"Alas, but we have no telephone here."

"Then I will call from the village. Now, if you'll excuse me, my car should be here soon, and I need to get home to see whether I still have a job."

* * * *

Berg left through the front gates, brushing dirt from the sleeves of his jacket and glad it had no bullets holes in it. His car was there, aimed down the mountain as if it could not wait to leave. He opened the back door and climbed in, to be greeted by a man dressed in black, his right hand resting on the seat and hidden by his thigh. "Have a seat, Mr. Robinson. I need to speak with you."

Moe answered as he sat and closed the door. "Well, you're as big as I am. Is there room enough for both of us? And, who might you be, sir?"

The car started in motion, and the man said, "I am Klaus Baer, and I wish to know who lives in the villa you just visited."

"I am not at liberty to say."

"I assure you that you will tell me what I want to know."

"Let me guess. You are an officer in the Gestapo, you have all the airport drivers under contract to inform you about any curious-looking visitors, and the hand hidden from my sight is holding a pistol. Am I correct in that?"

"You are a direct man. Let me also be direct." He raised the gun and pointed it a Berg. "I am indeed with the Gestapo, and you will tell me who is in that house, or I shall be forced to kill you."

"There is no need for that. I went there to visit an artist. She is reputed to be an exceptional talent, and I'm trying to get the rights to display her work before another museum beats me to it."

The driver pulled the car to a stop at the same spot where he had left Berg, and Baer said, "You insult me with you lies. I know you left this car at this very spot and scaled the rocks to gain access to the grounds. There would be no reason for that, if you were only trying to see an artist. No, Mr. Robinson, we have had this villa under surveillance for some time, and we know Pope Pius is there."

"Then you know more than I do. But, if you're so sure he's there, then why ask me? I have no interest in the man, unless he has paintings to offer."

"Get out."

Berg pushed the door open and crossed the road with Baer behind him and a Luger pressed against his back. "Where are we going?"

"Somehow you managed to find a way over a bare, rock face of this mountain without falling to your death. You will show me the path you took."

"Sure, I'd be glad to and, once I've done that, will you take me to the airport?"

"Of course. I have no reason to harm you, if you cooperate."

Berg led him over rugged ground and past thickets to a narrow ledge. He pointed up the hill. "Do you see the series of outcroppings down there to the left?" Baer nodded. "That's the route I took, but are you sure you want to lose your life for this?"

"I will not be the one to make the climb. We have people for that."

"No, no, I didn't mean risk your life climbing. I mean lose your life right now. We both know you're not going to let me leave here alive, and I can't allow to just kill me."

"You have no choice in the matter. The only person in danger of losing his life is you, Mr. Robinson. You forget that I hold the gun."

"I would choose to disagree with you. You see, my name isn't Robison. It's Berg, and I was a professional athlete with extremely quick hands and the reflexes of an athlete. If you will give the gun to me, I will spare your life."

"You are a stupid . . ." Berg slapped the gun aside, and a shot ricocheted off the ground, as he spun on his heel and drove his elbow into Baer's face. The big Nazi reeled, and Moe kicked him off the ledge. The body bounced three times before disappearing into a chasm. "Sorry about that, Klaus, but I warned you, and I won't let you kill that good man. Now, I'll have your driver take me to the airport, so I can make my phone call before I kick his ass."

* * * *

His gray hat shielded his head from the chill of a cool, foggy morning, and he plucked it off when he entered Q Building. The walk to the elevator in the back of the building was becoming familiar now, like the tunnel leading from the dressing room to the dugout at Fenway Park. Months passed from his first trip to the Balkans, with a short, unauthorized detour to Switzerland, and his return to Washington. And, now a year was behind him, a year of mundane existence in the doldrums of bureaucracy, but also a year with Stella, and that made it worthwhile. Still, the war raged, and he sat in Washington, watching and waiting for his chance to do something.

The fragrance of freshly-perked coffee welcomed him to the third floor and followed him to his office. And, there he found a note on his desk.

Please come see me.

Donovan

"Well, I wonder what this is about." He dropped his hat on the desk, stuffed the note into his pocket, and walked three doors down the hall to Bill Donovan's office. The secretary waved him through and pulled the door shut behind him.

Donovan peered over the top of a file he was reading and said, "Have a seat, Moe." Berg sank into an overstuffed, leather chair and waited. Donovan laid the folder on his desk and set his glasses beside it. "Let me start by reminding you of your training course and the fiasco at the aircraft factory."

"How could I forget, when you keep telling me? I know I screwed up, even for a rookie agent."

"We don't call ourselves agents anymore. We think operative is better, but, whatever we call the job, you can't make that kind of mistake on your next assignment. If you do, they'll torture you to death, and the Nazis are very proficient at torture."

"And, what is that assignment?"

"The report you filed on your time in Brazil says you met with a contact from MI6, and she told you about Werner Heisenberg and Otto Hahn. Tell me what you know about them."

"I know they're involved with Germany's project to develop a super weapon. Hahn has worked on the principles of fission for nearly a decade without perfecting it. With that kind of time investment and no results, his interest might be fading. But, Heisenberg is brilliant, and he is more patient than Hahn."

"Heisenberg may be the guy, but we can't get at him. He lives in the village of Hechingen, near the Black Forest in the southern part of Germany, and he is under heavy guard twenty-four hours a day. We'd like to capture him, but I suppose bombing his house would work as well. I know that sounds heartless, but they say he's an atheist, so maybe it isn't so bad."

"That's not what I read about him. I've looked at every file and European newspaper I can get my hands on, and he sounds like a very dedicated family man. He dotes on his children. It appears he is a Lutheran. When he was asked about God, he said, 'The first gulp from the glass of natural sciences will turn you into an atheist, but at the bottom of the glass, God is waiting for you.' You'd probably work on the bomb too, if they held a gun to your daughter's head. He deserves better than to have his family killed in a bombing raid."

"So do the families in London, but that doesn't stop Hitler from pounding the hell out of them every night. But then, we're not Hitler. And, before we resort to drastic measures, we want you to go to Italy. We've liberated parts of the country, enough for you to have access to a few scientists, like Edoardo Amaldi and perhaps as many as a dozen more. See whether you can convince them to defect and move to the US. And, while you're at it, pump them for anything they know about the bomb project."

"When do I leave?"

"Day after tomorrow. Treadwell is already there, posing as a worker in a bakery."

"That's good to know, but I can't operate under someone's thumb. He's going to have to let me do what I need to do without interference. If I'm going to get myself killed over there, it isn't going to be because someone got in my way, and that includes Mr. Treadwell."

"That's pretty bold, but it's fair. We'll get word to Treadwell that he is to lend you support as you need it, but the responsibility is yours. Now, there is a second part of this assignment. Hitler has removed Wilhelm Canaris as head of Abwehr. We think he got wind of how Canaris helped us foil the plot to assassinate Pope Pius."

"Yeah, I know how hard all you guys worked on that."

"Be a team player, Moe. Now, as I was trying to say, before Canaris was demoted, he told us about a lens assembly factory, the Galileo Company, near Florence."

"That could be interesting. Lens assembly has processes similar to those needed to compress fissionable materials, an essential part of making the bomb."

"Exactly. I see you've been doing your homework. The problem is that Florence is still in occupied Italy. When you get to Rome, Treadwell will introduce you to an OSS captain, Max Carson. Captain Carson's men have been making nighttime excursion into occupied territory, looking for fuel and ammo dumps. They will provide you with a German officer's uniform and identity papers, and they'll help you get somewhere close to Florence. After that, you're on your own. How you get access to the factory and what you do when you get there will be up to you."

"Is Treadwell the contact to transmit the information back to you?"

"Yes, assuming he doesn't get killed in the meantime. And, there's one more thing, Moe, and I almost never say this. The second part of the assignment is optional. If you don't feel ready for it, we'll get someone else."

Berg grinned. "Are you worried about me, Bill?"

"Hell, no. I'm worried about the mission. We'll only get one chance to determine whether this place is helping with the bomb. We don't want to risk the lives of our pilots to bomb a place that's making spectacles."

"That's comforting to know. It may take a few days to establish myself in the community, maybe have dinner with the plant manager before I inspect his factory. One thing I learned at Glenn Martin is that showing up unannounced raised suspicion and, if the Nazis catch me, I won't be able to blame it on J. Edgar."

"One more thing. Do you still have the film you shot when you played baseball in Japan?"

"Yes, it's in a filing cabinet in my office."

"Good. We have a meeting in an hour in the main conference room, and I'd like for you to bring it."

"Okay, but who am I showing it to?"

"There will be a few of us, but the person with the most interest will be Lieutenant Colonel Jimmy Doolittle. He's been training a group of pilots in South Carolina, bombing the crap out of some little island in one of their lakes. He'd like to see your film. He and his boys will be paying Tokyo a visit soon, a little greeting for what the Japanese did at Pearl."

* * * *

The next thirty-six hours were precious to Moe and Stella, and they didn't want to spend them in her apartment or his hotel room. There was nothing sexy about their heavy coats and warm hats, as they walked the narrow beach on Sandy Neck to the sound of waves crashing over rocks and the distant cry of sea birds. This day, this last day together for what could be a very long time, was about holding hands, tender kisses, and sharing a deep devotion for each other. They spread a plaid blanket on the dunes and sat next to each other, quietly staring over Cape Cod Bay, and their lives paused. There was no Hitler, no OSS, nothing to pull them apart. Stella took his gloved hand in hers, and they lay back on the blanket. "Tell me everything will be all right, Moe. Tell me like you mean it."

"It will be. I have it on good authority that good health and prosperity await in my future. At least that's what my horoscope in the Globe said this morning."

"Well, I hope it's right. I wish you'd tell me where you're going, so I could keep track of what's going on there."

"You know better. I'll write you as often as I can, but the letters have to go through the military mail, so there won't be postmarks. It's important that you don't know and that no one outside the family knows about you. You'll be safer. Use my mother's return address for your letters and send them through my office in Washington. They'll find me."

She squeezed his hand and sighed. "Let's not talk about that anymore. Let's talk about happy things."

"Okay, what would make you happy?"

"I'd like to have a baby."

"A baby? You mean a little, fuzzy headed Moe Jr. with beady eyes and feet like a chimpanzee?"

"I don't care what size his feet are. I regret not marrying you two years ago. If I had, I could've had our child to keep me company while you're gone, and you'd have someone to come home to."

"I have you to come home to. That's enough. But, I'll look into it while I'm overseas. They say Hitler has people working on how to propagate the master race, blond hair, blue eyes, the whole Arian package. Maybe I can find a way to have the baby look like you instead of me."

"Our baby would be beautiful if his mug was the shape of an elephant's butt."

"Whoa, that's quite an image." He pulled her hand up and shook his head with it. "There, rattle that picture out of my brain." Then he kissed her. "I'll bring you an engagement ring that will knock your socks off, even if I have to steal it."

"You do that, and I'll have the Justice of the Peace waiting at the airport when you get back."

"Now, that's what I like to hear. We're going to have a long life together, Stella, a long, happy life."

Chapter Seven

The ache in his heart was accompanied by aches in his hips and back, as Moe Berg flew from Washington to Newfoundland and on to Scotland, London, and Madrid before reaching Rome. The lavish Hotel Excelsior, spared most of the ravishes of war, welcomed him like a favorite uncle who had been gone too long. He feasted on oysters, drank wine, and slept on satin sheets. A breakfast of eggs, sausage, and strong coffee was his last vision of what Rome had once been, before he walked the streets toward the Colosseum and saw what it now was, buildings crumbling from artillery fire and the stark, desperate look on the faces of people who seemed not sure whether the Nazis would be back, some perhaps hoping they would. He reached the ancient venue, where Caesars watched races and acts of Barbary, and he found Treadwell sitting on the front row. "I expected to see you in an apron."

"If you had come to the bakery at five o'clock this morning, you would have. And, I have to get back, so let's make this quick." He pointed across the arena. "Exit over there, and you'll find a car waiting for you. It will take you where you need to go. First, you will see Edoardo Amaldi. We've only had access to him and Otto Hahn for a few days, but you won't be the first one to try to convince them to join us. Amaldi doesn't trust us and he adamantly refused to defect to America without being forced. If we kidnap him, any chance of his cooperating with us would be lost. You'll see Hahn sometime next week."

"When do I meet Captain Carson?"

"I thought you might pass on that part of the mission, but I'm glad you didn't. Carson and his men are in the process of relocating their camp. It may be three or four days, even a week, before we know where they are. When we know, I'll get in touch. Do you want a weapon?"

"Not yet. The mission with the scientists is diplomatic. My being armed could arouse their suspicion and queer the whole deal."

"Your driver has a rifle, but be careful. You never know when you'll run into a German patrol. What's you cover story?"

Berg took a single diamond from his pocket. "I am a dealer in precious stones, whose business was destroyed by American bombers. I'm trying to get to my home in the country and see my wife. When they ask for my papers, this little baby will accidently fall out, a convenient distraction."

Treadwell shook his hand and said, "Good luck, Berg. I'll see you in a couple of days."

"When you come, could you bring a few croissants?"

"You should be in show business. You really should, only not as a comedian."

* * * *

Dear Stella,

I am safe, but I miss you so. Things are so different than the last time I was in Europe. Destruction is everywhere, families torn apart, lives cut short. And yet, in the midst of all this, there is beauty. In spite of our best efforts to destroy each other, the rivers and mountains survive it all and shine as they have for eons. They mock our futility and our vanity.

I expect to be home before very long, perhaps a few weeks. Then we can be together. My heart longs for you. Please call Mama and let her know I'm all right. She worries for no reason. And, give Ethel my love.

Thinking of you always,

Moe

The metal gate stood open, its hinges broken, and half the stones in the path to the front door were painted with crude swastikas. Berg shifted the weight of a cardboard box from one arm to the other and turned back to his driver. "Flip these stones over while I'm inside. This is an Italian home now." The woman who answered the door looked different than Moe expected. Edoardo Amaldi's file said his wife was thirty three, but she wore the worry lines of an older woman. "Good day. You must be Ginestra. I'm Moe Berg, here to see Dr. Amaldi. I believe he is expecting me."

"Please come in. He is in the study, just down there, but you are wasting your time. I have been married to him for twelve years. He will not abandon his country in time of war."

"I understand, but perhaps I could have a few moments with him." She gestured toward a doorway at the end of the hall, and Berg nodded a thank you as he left her. He found a clean-shaven man sitting on the floor, smeared with grease, wrench in hand, working on an old bicycle. "Dr. Amaldi?"

"Would you hand that screwdriver to me?"

"Sure, here you go. Can I get you anything else?"

"You could get out of my house and leave me in peace, but you won't do that, will you, Mr. Berg?"

"Did the Nazis leave you in peace?" Amaldi didn't answer. "No, they harassed you and your family. I'm surprised they didn't load you in the back of a truck and haul you to Berlin in chains or, failing that, just shoot you dead."

The young man lowered his tools and his tone softened. "They would have, if they could've found us. When I heard the Americans were approaching, I hid my family in the woods. We lived like animals for nearly a week, but we survived." He pointed toward the box under Berg's arm. "Have you come to put me in chains?"

Moe set the box on the floor and opened the top. A pair of nylon hose sizzled, as he lifted them out. "They're not chains, Doctor Amaldi. With your permission, I brought these for your wife, and I have a side of beef and chocolates."

"Do you think to bribe me with nylons and candy?"

"Not at all. This is my way of thanking you for allowing me the hospitality of your home, and I hope you will invite me to share in roasting this beef for dinner tonight."

"It has been many weeks since we have tasted fresh meat. The Germans took everything." He smiled. "Except for one bottle of wine. We buried it under a stump. We will share your beef, but you must share our wine."

"It doesn't happen to be white burgundy, does it?"

"But, of course. What else would an Italian risk his life for?"

* * * *

Amaldi's youngest daughter sat next to Berg, as her mother cleared the dishes from the table. "How old are you, little one?" he asked.

"Six."

"I have a daughter about your age. Her name is Ethel, and she likes to roller skate."

"Are you going to take my father away?"

"Why do you ask me that?"

"The Nazi men came to take him, but we hid. I got all itchy in the woods."

"Yes, your father told me about that. And, no, I didn't come to take him away from you. I'm from America. Have you heard about my country?"

"Only a little. It's on the other side of the world. Your soldiers sent the Nazis away."

He smiled and patted the side of her face. "America is a beautiful land, far away from the Nazis. No one would ever harm you there. If your father wants to come there, you and your family would come with him. We'd fly you there on a big airplane. Would you like that?"

Amaldi put a match to his pipe and muttered, "You may leave the table now, Elena. Mr. Berg and I need to talk."

She dropped out of her chair and walked away quietly. "You have a lovely family, Edoardo. Is it all right if I call you Edoardo?"

"You have fed my family. You may call me whatever you wish."

"Thank you, and please call me Moe." Berg sniffed the air. "Is that Cavendish you're smoking?"

"Cavendish, yes, with burley and a touch of latakia. My father smoked a pipe, and it was his favorite blend. Now, it is mine."

"Have you heard from your father lately?"

"Not for a long time. He fled the country when the Fascists took over. My mother is a Jew, and politics being what they are, he thought it safer to get her out of the country."

"If you like, we could find them for you, even get them to America, if they're in danger. There are many opportunities for professors of mathematics in our universities. He would do well there."

"You know a lot about my family, Mr. Berg, uh, Moe. You are very different from the man who came yesterday."

Berg lifted his wine glass from the table and leaned back in his chair. "Different in what way?"

"He came with soldiers to protect him. Their rifles frightened my children. He told me Enrico Fermi has fled the country and I should do the same. And, you call my wife by her given name. You spend time with my children and talk of a better life for them. There is no threat in your voice."

"Well, your family has welcomed me, like more than a guest. I, too, am separated from my parents. Both were taken prisoner when Germany captured Poland. Like your mother, we are Jews, and I fear for their safety. I fear for everyone's safety if Hitler manages to develop an atomic weapon. If our troops can't clear the German Army out of Italy, they'll be back, and we won't be able to protect Ginestra or Eleana or any of your children. Come with us now, while there is time."

Amaldi tamped his tobacco and relit it. Smoke plumed around his head, and he took his time before answering. "I will consider all the things you have said. Will you take my family to safety, if I don't go with you?"

"I'd like to say yes, but I would never lie to you. I would do everything in my power to help them, but my government wants you. Whether I could convince them to move your family without you, I just couldn't say."

"But, if I knew my family was safe, the Nazis would have no leverage to force me to help them. Is that not of value to your government?"

"Indeed it is, Edoardo. I will do my very best to find a place for them on one of our planes. And, we'll relocate them somewhere that has other Italians, so they feel at home, maybe Chicago. I have friends there."

"Then, I will speak with my wife this evening. Visit us again tomorrow, and I'll have an answer for you."

Berg drained the last of his wine from the glass, set it back onto the table, and stood. "I will talk with my people tonight and see you for lunch. My hotel has fresh eggs and sausage. Whatever your decision, we can at least have one, good last meal together."

"That is kind of you. I must return to the university in the morning, but I always arrive home at one fifteen. I will see you then."

Amaldi walked him to the door, and Moe pressed his hat onto his head. "Let your heart lead you, Edoardo. The fate of the world is at stake."

* * * *

Evening covered the city, and Berg made his same trek to front-row seats of the Colosseum. "How did you come out with Amaldi?" Treadwell asked.

"I'm having lunch with his family tomorrow, and he'll give me his answer then."

"But, you were supposed to get him today."

"Be patient, Woody."

"Don't call me that. I'm your superior officer."

"Yeah, well you can file that under the heading of 'I Don't Care'. When my life and the lives of those children are at stake, rank means nothing to me. We're going to play this my way."

"I'll send a box of croissants to your hotel room. You can take them with you tomorrow."

"That would be very nice. Thank you. I expect him to say he wants to stay in Italy and have his family taken to the US."

"We can't do that. We'll have to kidnap him. If the Nazis retake the country, they'll grab him quick. They won't make the same mistake twice."

"That may be, but he won't help them if his family is safe. He could tell them we took his family, and we're holding them as hostages. It gives him a viable excuse. I don't like the idea of kidnapping the guy. It doesn't bode

131

well for cooperation. We're not in the business of threatening children to force it either and, besides, I've already promised him we'd do it."

"You have no authority to, oh shit. Okay, do what you can. If we hold onto Italy, it won't matter. You won't get to see Otto Hahn. We thought we had him on his way out of Germany, but he was arrested in Belgium. And, Carson's men got caught up in a firefight outside Arezzo. We're not sure where they are or if they're even alive. So, you'll have to wait to check out the Galileo Company."

"I thought I was going to be out of here next week."

"Did Wild Bill tell you that? Well, if he did, don't count on it. Those guys in Washington are out of touch with what goes on in the field. There's a war going on, and we've got work to do. There are more than a dozen scientists, spread all over Italy, that we need you to convince to join us. You're a long way from going home. Oh, and when it comes to Amaldi, please don't promise him anything else we can't back up, like a role in the next Clark Gable movie."

"I'd never do that. I prefer Gary Cooper."

"That just isn't funny."

"Well, there's something you can do for me." He pulled a paper from his breast pocket and handed it to Treadwell. "Contact our people in London and have them cable this message to me."

"Okay, I'm not even going to ask why you would send yourself a message."

"It isn't for me. It's for Amaldi."

* * * *

Moe stepped out of his car carrying a basket of eggs, two pounds of sausage, and a bottle of milk. He tapped the bottom of the door with the tip of his shoe, and Ginestra answered. "Oh, Mr. Berg. You must have misunderstood.

It is but ten o'clock, and my husband will not be home until one fifteen. He is very prompt."

"My stars, he told me that. I am such an idiot. Please forgive me. I'll wait in the car."

"No, no, you must not do that. Please come inside."

"You are so kind, but the day is already hot. Could we sit under the tree for a while? I brought milk. Perhaps we could cool it in the well until Dr. Amaldi gets home."

She stepped out, pulling the door shut behind her. They crossed the yard to the side of the house and sat on a bench under a large, ancient oak. "It has been a long time since I sat under this tree. When we first moved into this house, Edoardo and I would come here every evening. He smoked his pipe, and we talked for hours." She raised a droll smile and said, "Of course, that was before the children came. Now, we scarcely have time for that."

"You should take time."

` "Do you have a wife at home, Mr. Berg? Do you miss her?"

"Call me Moe, and, no, I don't have a wife, per se. I do have a girl. And, yes, I do miss her. She teaches children to play piano and violin in New York. Her students are from five to twelve years old, much like your children."

"Uga, our oldest son, plays piano, or he did. When the Germans came, they burned his school and shot his teacher. Perhaps he will play again one day."

"He could be playing within a week in America."

"I wondered when you would get to that. It is no mistake that you came early, is it?"

"No. I wanted some time with you alone. You would have a wonderful life in America, you, Edoardo, and your children. They would all go to universities, and you'd have time to sit under a tree with your husband. Time together without wondering when the next bomb will fall or whether an assassin has been sent to kill your family."

"Oh, it sounds like a dream, this America. No more Hitler, no more fascists. Peace and family. Is there really such a place on this earth, Moe Berg? Or is it a fantasy?"

"It's real, Ginestra. I won't tell you America is perfect. We have our problems. But, I can promise you a home and opportunities for your children that they won't find here. Please don't stay here and see little Elena trampled under some Nazi's boot."

She plowed her fingers through her long, tousled hair and moaned, "If it were my choice, I would leave this minute, but Edoardo will not forsake Italy. It's his home, and I will not leave him, no matter the consequences."

"Very well. Then I shall leave the basket and the milk for you to enjoy with him when he comes home. And, please tell him that I have one request, and I must insist on it."

"What is that?"

"He will be my guest for dinner tonight at the Arturo Restaurant. Tell him that refusal is not the act of a friend."

"I will tell him, but you are wasting your time and money, if you think you can convince my husband to leave his country. He will never do it, not even for the man who brings him milk and eggs."

* * * *

Amaldi checked his hat at the front of the restaurant, nodded to Berg, and walked to his table. "A linen tablecloth, fine china, and gold-plated flatware. I'm surprised the Germans left any of this."

"We have ways of providing for our honored guests, Edoardo. Please have a seat." Berg motioned for the waiter to pour wine, as Amaldi lowered his lean body into his chair. "I took the liberty of ordering for both of us. I hope you don't mind."

"Not at all. Judging by what I've seen so far, I expect dinner will be no less impressive. But, I must say I feel strange dining in such elegance while my family is left to meager fare."

"I thought of that, and the kitchen is preparing portions for each member of your family. Oh, and I brought a few things." He took a bag from beneath the table and set it on the extra chair. "I have a few gifts for the children, just to say thank you for the hospitality your family extended to me."

"But, there is no need to . . ."

"Please, please, don't deny me this small gesture of gratitude. And, there is a bottle of perfume for Genestra. I'll let you look all this over when you get home, but there is one item I'd like to share with you now." He plucked a leather pouch from the sack and tossed it onto the table in front of Amaldi. "Cavendish and burley with a touch of latakia. Did you bring your pipe?"

"I go nowhere without it."

"Then you must smoke a bowl tonight and tell me how you like it, but first let's have dinner."

Three waiters catered to their every request with plates of roast lamb, oysters, grilled asparagus, and fresh bread. As dinner ended, the waiters cleared the table, and Amaldi finished his third glass of wine. "You have been very kind to us, Moe. I cannot tell you how much it means to me to know my family will be safe."

"And, you will be safe too, Edoardo."

"I hope that is true, but only if the Germans do not return and overpower your troops. But, that is the chance I must take for my country."

"Actually, it isn't." Berg handed him a cablegram. "I got this from our office in London. Please read it."

"Very well. Here, let me get my spectacles. Yes, there. It says, 'Located Goldilocks' cabin. Can deal in three days upon request.' I assume this is code, but what does it mean?"

"When Goldilocks went into the cabin, she found Mama Bear and Papa Bear. That's code for your parents. We found them, and our people can affect a rescue within three days of the time I request it."

Amaldi's face quivered, and he reached for a napkin to wipe his eyes. "That is wonderful news. I have been so worried. I thought they might be dead." The room sank to an awkward silence. "And, now it is clear. There is a price for their rescue."

"It's a dangerous mission, and we won't risk the lives of our people without a good reason. That reason is you."

"I thought as much."

"My driver will take you home. You will take your family dinner and gifts. Collect the things you hold most dear, and my man will take all of you to a landing strip in Naples. By morning, you'll be on your way to Madrid and from there to London and New York and, finally, Chicago. If you choose not to go, we'll keep our promise to take your wife and children, but we won't take the risk for your parents, if you're not on that plane."

Amaldi sat for a moment, loaded his pipe, and fired it to a rich billow of white smoke. "You are most persuasive. Call your driver."

"He's waiting for you in front of the restaurant." They both stood and shook hands. "You're doing the right thing, my friend." Amaldi simply smiled and walked out. As
Berg sat back down, a man rose from the next table and

sat beside him. "Now you know why I needed that cablegram."

Treadwell crossed his legs and folded his arms. "How did you go about finding his parents without my knowing about it?"

"Hell, I don't know where his parents are."

"Moe, he'll be furious when he figures this out."

"That he will, Woodrow. So, you don't need to waste any time finding out where they are. I suppose in a worst-case scenario, we could tell him the rescue mission failed. Throw in some details, like five of our men were killed in the attempt, and that way he'd feel like we made our best effort."

"You may not feel so clever by the end of the week."

"I take it you've located Captain Carson and his men."

"Yes, and we're making arrangements now for you to rendezvous with them. It's no secret that you've been trying to recruit these scientists, and that's why we didn't hide your identity. Going behind enemy lines is different. Your code name will be Romulus. Carson's men were ambushed last week, and we think there might be a double agent among them. Learn all you can about the Galileo Company, but protect yourself."

"That's what I do best. I hope."

* * * *

Hi Moe,

No, it's not your mother, in spite of the return address (Ha Ha). I've picked up some extra music students since you left. It keeps me busy, and the money comes in handy. But, the nights are very long and lonely. I miss having you beside me in our bed. Sometimes I wake up looking for you. I count the days, but weeks pass so slowly. I'd hoped you'd be home by now.

Ethel was promoted to supervise the other teachers at her school. She skates down the hallways to check on their classes. I'm getting to know her better, and I think she likes me. Dr. Sam went to California. That's all I know. No one seems to keep in touch with him. Your mother is well and sends her love. Well, I should go now. I'm battling a cold, treating it with bourbon, so bedtime calls.

Don't forget your promise. Be safe.

Loving and missing you every day,
Stella

P.S. I thought of a name for when we have a baby –
Moella. Don't you love it?

Chapter Eight

His wingtip shoes and dark blue suit were ill fitted for traipsing through the woods in the dark, carrying a suitcase, but Berg pushed his way through scrub brush all the same until he heard a voice calling. "Stand where you are." He raised his hands to chest high and waited. "When did the cow jump over the moon?"

"Thirteen o'clock."

"Keep walking, and we'll meet you in the clearing just ahead." Moe held his hat in place, as he dodged tree limbs and stumbled over rocks to a modest camp and six armed men dressed in work shirts and trousers. The only one wearing a cap stepped forward and offered his hand. "I'm Max Carson. What shall we call you?"

"Romulus."

"All right. Can I offer you some dinner? We're running a cold camp, but we have Spam and crackers."

"No, thank you. I ate before I left the hotel. Captain, can we talk privately?"

He pulled back a tent flap and said, "Come in here. It's not your hotel, but it'll have to do." The shorter man passed through the opening with ease, but Berg had to shift sideways and stumble inside. He sat on a cot across from Carson. "I'm the only one here who knows your mission, and the only one who knows who you really are."

"I see you haven't forgotten Brazil."

"And, I haven't forgotten that you didn't turn me in to my superiors. I wouldn't be a captain now, if you had. Do you have a uniform and credentials?"

"In the suitcase, but I didn't see a staff car. They said you'd have one."

"We don't have it here."

He spread a map on the ground and pointed to a spot north of where they sat. "There's an Army camp about five miles from here, right there, and they have it. I'll take you and Stumpy there in my Jeep tomorrow."

"Stumpy?"

"He's the guy in the black coat, the one chewing tobacco. He'll pose as your driver. No German major would drive himself around."

"Yes, I learned that lesson the hard way. Does Stumpy speak German?"

"Don't worry about that. He'll stay by the car and keep his mouth shut."

"But, I do worry about it. If some Nazi soldier asks him for a smoke, what's he going to do? I'll tell you what he'll do. He'll get us both shot. No, we'll find someone at the camp who speaks German, and I mean fluent German."

"That's not easy to come by. What if they don't have anybody?"

" Sprechen sie Deutsch?"

"Ja, fließend Deutsch. But, you don't expect me to drive you. I have these men to look after."

"They'll look after themselves for the next few days. You're coming with me, and that's an order." Berg was no higher rank in the OSS than Carson, but only he knew that, and he was getting very good at contorting the truth. "We'll pick up the car tonight, and we'll change clothes once we're out of camp. I don't want anyone to see us drive out of there in German uniforms. It takes only one turncoat to blow our cover, and I'm not going to chance that."

"But, I don't have a uniform."

"In the suitcase. When I heard you were my contact, I had a corporal's uniform tailored to fit you. We even scuffed it up a bit to look like you've been wearing it for a while."

"All right, I'll go tell the men we're leaving and give them a few chores to keep them busy for a couple of days."

"And, tell Stumpy he's coming with us."

"I thought you didn't want him."

"When we get to the camp, we'll requisition something better than Spam, maybe even find some beer, and Stumpy can drive it back in the Jeep."

"They'll love you for that. I'll have Stumpy pick us up at the camp in three days. Is that long enough?"

"The timing should be right, but we won't be going back to the camp." He dragged his finger along the map. "We'll go in using this route, but we'll come out this way. I'm sure the Germans know where the camp is. If they figure us out before we get back, they could draw a bee line to it and run us down with a motorcycle and a machine gun. We'll take an alternate route, and your men can meet us at this point. Do you know it?"

"It's an old saw mill. We passed it last week."

"Good. Can we count on your men to be there?"

"I'd bet my life on it."

"You are betting your life, Max. We both are."

* * * *

Stumpy dropped his two passengers off and waited long enough for Berg to give him a gunny sack filled with potatoes, canned ham, and three bottles of beer. "What did you have to trade for that?" Carson asked.

"I told the sergeant in charge I was close to General Howard, and I could arrange for a weekend pass to Rome, if he gave me what I wanted."

"Have you actually met General Howard?"

"Not the one who is in charge of this regiment, but I did meet a colonel named Howard in Washington. I'm sure he's a general by now."

"Yeah, I'm sure he is. Well, while you were charming that sergeant, I talked to Captain Wilkinson. He says our staff car is parked down that way, just past the hospital tent. The keys are in it, and they filled the tank with diesel."

"I'm glad to hear that. Fuel is hard to come by. And, may I ask, what did you promise him in order to get it?"

"I didn't promise anything. I gave him three cigars, the last I had. And, I requisitioned these two rifles and half a dozen grenades."

"Well done, Max. There's a bridge about eight kilometers outside Florence. We'll stash the rifles and grenades there in case we need them. Now, let's go get our car." They trampled over mud and ruts cut into the ground by heavy trucks until they reached the hospital, and they stopped. "Do you know what that odor is?"

"All too well. It's the smell of open wounds and burned flesh. You never forget that once you've smelled it."

"Let's go in and speak to some of the men."

"Are you sure you want to do that? These places can be pretty gruesome."

"I'm sure, Max. I didn't come here just to sit in hotels and lie to scientists. I came to help with the war effort, and these men have given much more than I have. Yes, I need to see them." Berg set his suitcase at the entrance to the tent and walked from one cot to another, asking injured soldiers about their families and assuring them their wounds were not as bad as they really were. Whatever boyish inclinations remained in Moe Berg, those traits of innocence that clung to his soul were burned out in the light of broken bodies and dreams lost. Nothing remained unchanged.

* * * *

Long, narrow, dark roads brought them to Florence and to the one hotel that had not been shelled into rubble. But, every room was filled with officers ranking higher than Berg's phony major status. His best lies could not win him a room, but they did win him advice from the clerk to stay with a widow and her son at the edge of town. The house was small and inviting. The woman looked too old to have a teenage son, but she was pleasant, and her vacant bedroom was adequate for his needs. "I am sorry that we have but the one room, Major," she said. "I could put a blanket on the floor for your driver."

Berg glanced at Carson and said, "Don't worry about him. He can sleep in the car."

"As you like. I would offer you food, but all we have is cheese and bread."

He took a few Reichsmarks from his pocket and handed them to the woman. "Cheese and bread will be fine for tonight, but tomorrow you must rise early and buy more food. I will have sausages and eggs for breakfast with dark coffee. You will buy all these things and enough cheese and bread to replace what my man and I eat tonight."

"But, this is much more than enough to buy all that."

"You must keep the rest in case I have other needs."

"Yes, of course, thank you. Please sit at the table, and I will get your food." Berg and Carson sat down, and she placed a block of cheese and half a loaf of baked bread between them. When she had sliced them, she paused, opened a small cabinet, and took out a bottle of wine. "We have only part of a bottle, but your kindness deserves something better than water alone."

Berg barked an answer. "It is not kindness, fraulein. You have an officer of the Third Reich in your home, and you must tend to my needs. But, I do thank you for the wine."

The front door burst open, and Berg reached for his pistol. "Oh, please, please, it is only my son."

The boy snapped to attention, thrust his hand into the air, and said, "Heil Hitler!"

As much as Berg wanted to protect his cover, he could not bring himself to say those words. "Why does this child stand before me like a soldier, mocking the Fuhrer?"

"I mean no disrespect, sir."

His mother stepped between them. "Salvatore joined the Hitler Youth two months ago. He is trying to be a good soldier." Her face bespoke of worry. "I think he will be called to the Army soon."

Moe gestured toward Carson. "Get up and let this boy sit down." He waited until Carson rose, and the youngster replaced him at the table. "So, you cannot offer a proper salute and you want to be a German soldier?"

"Yes, Major. I want it more than anything."

"And, why do you want this thing?"

The boy stumbled as he answered. "Because, it's, I want, a soldier is brave. He is courageous. I want to help kill the Americans."

"What have the Americans done to you that makes you want to kill them?"

"Vincent's father says they invaded Italy and they will trample over us all. They are a vile people of mixed races."

"Vincent is your friend?"

"My very best friend. We joined the Hitler Youth together, and we're going to drive the Americans out of Italy."

Berg looked up at the mother and asked, "Is this what you want for your child, to be a German soldier and kill the Americans?" She lowered her gaze, and that told him everything he needed to know. "Madame, bring me some paper and a pen and ink." She went back to the cabinet, found what he needed and set them on the table. Berg talked as he wrote. "Germans are the finest people in the world, and the German soldier is the most excellent warrior in the history of mankind. He is strong and fears nothing. His mind sees the battle before it happens, and he brings his enemies to their knees. And, you, who stumbles in his speech, who quakes at the sight of my uniform, you would be that soldier?"

"Yes, Major, I would."

Berg breathed on the paper to dry the ink and handed it to the mother. "Take this, woman, and give it to the commander of the Hitler Youth. It is my order, finding this boy totally unfit for military duty. He is to be expelled from the Hitler Youth and never to be considered for the Army." Salvatore tried to speak, but Moe slapped his swagger stick on the table. "Get out of my sight, before I have you flogged for the imposter you are." He slapped the table again. "And, stop that crying." Moe poured himself a glass of wine, as the boy shrank into a back room, but the mother stayed. "Do you have something to say to me?"

"Yes, Major. Thank you. I think you saved my boy's life."

"Make sure you don't forget my eggs."

* * * *

She did not forget his eggs or the sausages or the coffee. Berg wanted to leave her more money and to reassure her about the liberation soon to find its way to Florence, but he didn't know her well enough. She cared

145

about her son, but that didn't mean she wasn't loyal to the Fascists or the Nazis. So, he left her with a list of the foods he wanted for dinner and sharp instructions that his bed have fresh sheets for his return that night. Carson parked the car next to the curb in front of the hotel that had refused them lodging. "Do you want me to stay by the car, Major?"

Even in this private moment, Berg stayed in character. "You will go to the factory and tell the plant manager I want to see him. Tell him to come here at noon, and I will meet him in the dining room. If I am not there when he arrives, he is to wait." The long, black car drove away, as Berg walked into the hotel lobby, with a newspaper stuffed under his arm, and stopped at the desk. "Do you have a room where I can read in quiet?"

"Yes, sir. You will find it on the left side of the hall, just past the elevator. And, I apologize that the elevator does not work anymore."

"I have no need for the elevator. You will tell your people to bring me a pot of coffee and reserve a table for myself and a guest for lunch."

"Right away."

Berg tapped his cap bill with his swagger stick. "Good." He found the reading room and a comfortable chair, but he was not alone. Two Italian lieutenants and a German captain sat, smoking cigarettes, on the opposite side of the room. Berg spread the paper over his lap, and nothing was said until the waiter brought his coffee on a tray.

"That coffee smells wonderful." The captain said.

"It does." He took a sip from his cup. "And, it tastes as good as it smells."

"We have recently returned from the front, and came here looking for a room, but they have none. Were you at the front, sir?"

"Why do you insist on talking to me when I am trying to read, Captain?"

"My apologies, Major, but your accent is strange to me. I thought it rude to ask you what part of Germany is your home, and perhaps the name of your regiment might have told me that. "

Berg wondered what he had missed. Was there something in his inflection that drew suspicion? If he ignored the question, would it make the captain more suspicious? "I do find you rude, but at times we must be rude to do our jobs. I find it odd that three soldiers, who claim to have come from the front, are sitting in a hotel with nothing better to do than ask foolish questions of superior officers." He jerked his Luger from its holster and pointed it at them. "Now, Captain, or whoever you are, what part of Germany is your home?"

"Aschen, a small town west of Cologne."

"Do you think to teach me geography? I know where Aschen is. My home is Siegen, in the mountains. You live less than two hundred kilometers from Siegen, and you do not know our accent? How can that be?"

"Oh, Siegen, of course. My, uh, my wife has an uncle from Siegen, and he has the same accent. How stupid of me not to recognize it."

"Hmm, yes, I don't know whether to believe you or shoot you. Either would serve the Reich equally well."

The soldiers all stood and saluted. "If you will allow it, sir, we will leave you to your coffee and your newspaper, begging you forgiveness for the intrusion."

Berg waved his pistol toward the door, and they filed out. He put his Luger away, sipped his coffee, and whispered, "There's nothing like a loaded gun to win a man's respect and cooperation."

* * * *

Lunch was disappointing with meager servings of chicken and rice. Like everyone in Florence, the hotel was struggling to keep a supply of food, and Berg knew that. Still, he had to maintain the image of a Nazi major. He railed at the waiter, demanding he go back to the kitchen and return with a chicken fat enough to satisfy his German appetite. The waiter hurried away, as a short, stocky man arrived. Berg stood and clicked his heels. "You must be Dr. Martinez."

"Paolo Martinez, plant manager of Galileo. Thank you for inviting me to lunch, Major Heinrich." He offered his hand, but Berg refused it.

"Please sit. I have a few questions for you before I visit your factory." He waited for Martinez to take his chair before sitting down. "We have received reports that your production rates are inadequate for our needs."

"But, we have produced everything asked of us. I work the people twelve-hour days."

"And, do you work a crew at night?"

"We have not needed to work at night."

"Then you must consider it, if you cannot increase productivity of your workers. Do you have Jews working there?"

"Only those who have essential skills. We lost so many craftsmen to the war effort that I have been forced to use Jewish labor."

"I will judge that for myself this afternoon, when I inspect your facility. But, for now, we shall have a glass of schnapps and some lunch. I hope you like overcooked chicken."

* * * *

Carson and Berg followed Dr. Martinez's car through the gate and to the front of a tan-colored, stone building, but only after showing their credentials twice and having their car thoroughly searched. Berg left Carson with the car and climbed three steps to the entrance. Martinez held the front door ajar and said, "Let me apologize again, but I'm sure you understand the need for strict security."

"Of course. I would expect no less."

He motioned toward the factory floor and described the processes as they walked down the production line. "We receive raw materials in the form of sheets of glass, each of a particular thickness, depending on the product to be made. You can see here that we cut those into ingots, using finely honed cutting tools. The ingots are heated and formed under pressure into concave lenses at this station, and they are polished over there at the end of the preparation line."

"I'd like to stop for a moment and see a full cycle of the forming process." He folded his arms, with his swagger stick resting in the crook of his elbow, and put his photographic memory to work. "Yes, yes, this is the standard process, but how much pressure do you put on the ingot?"

"That I am not allowed to say. I would need an order from the local commander to discuss those particulars. Shall I call him?"

"That isn't necessary. It was simply a curiosity, not worth bothering a general." They crossed the aisle to the assembly line. "What kinds of products do you manufacture, Doctor?"

"We build a full line of range finders, periscopes, search lights, and telescopes. They are the finest products of their kind in all of Italy."

"And, if we were to ask you to produce a new product, how quickly could you staff another crew?"

"That depends on the complexity of the product. As I told you earlier, it is not easy to find skilled craftsmen in these times. Oh, would you excuse me, Major? My foreman seems to have a problem." Martinez walked slowly down the line and spoke to a man dressed in a white shirt. The man glanced at Berg, turned, and left the production floor. Martinez returned just as slowly as he had left. "We seem to be having some fluctuation in our compressed air lines. I sent my man to call the maintenance people to look into it. It is the way we do things, nothing left till tomorrow that can be fixed today."

"That is the way it must be. Now, let me return to my question. The Reich will have need of some, shall we say, new products soon, and those could be made using these same types of processes. If you are unable to find more craftsmen, we may need to call on you to stop lens production in order to manufacture these new products."

"It would need to be a very special product, if we are to deny the military of periscopes and range finders."

"It is. Have you read General Goebel's most recent pamphlet?"

"If you mean the one about the atomic torpedo, yes, I have, and it would be our honor to assist with that project. My humble factory could be part of history."

"Good. I have seen enough to satisfy my curiosity about your facility. Will you join me for dinner at the hotel tonight?"

"I'd love to."

"Then I'll see you at seven. If you will show me back to my car, I will contact Berlin with a good report."

"That is very kind of you, Major. Please, step right this way."

Something felt very wrong. Berg wanted to run out, but he couldn't. He took confident strides to the exit door, bade his host goodbye, and climbed into the back seat of the car. When the factory door closed, he said, "Get us out of here, Max. I think he sent his foreman to call the Gestapo." Carson put the car in motion and stopped at the gate to have it searched again. Berg sensed the guard was stalling. *He's waiting for the Gestapo to get here. I can't have that.* "How many times must you search an empty boot?" he called, but there was no answer. Berg stepped out of the car and walked around the rear fender. He shoved his pistol into the guard's chest, forced him into the trunk, and hurried back to his seat. "Okay, ease out of here and then step on it."

Carson didn't have to be told twice. Once they cleared the crest of a small hill, he opened the engine to full speed. "Where are we going?"

"Take the road east until we cross the bridge and then turn south. Head for the rendezvous site, as quickly as you can. This thing isn't built for speed, so we need to put as much distance between us and them as we can. We can blow the bridge with the grenades we hid there, if they don't catch us first."

"I've got the accelerator to the floor. Hold on tight." It felt like Carson hit every rut in the road, as they fled down a battered, dirt road. Then Berg's worst fear rolled up behind them on two motorcycles with machine guns slung over their shoulders.

"Push it, Max."

"I am pushing it. They're too fast."

"There, the bridge. When you cross it, swing this thing sideways." The long car clattered over the wooden bridge and slung dirt, as Carson spun it around. They climbed out and opened fire with their pistols. The German soldiers rode into the trees, took cover behind a large rock, and returned the favor. Bullets stung the body of the car in rapid fashion, driving Berg and Carson to the ground. "See if you can get to the grenades, Max. I'll try to draw their fire." Moe duck walked to the rear fender and fired five shots, while Carson crawled toward the bridge. Both machine guns riddled the trunk. Berg sat behind the front wheel and reloaded his pistol. "Oh, shit. I should've brought more bullets. Come on, Max." He wondered if Carson was dead, and he knew he'd be next. Again he rose and he fired the last of his ammunition. When he sank back to the ground, he saw a welcome face. "Thank God. I thought they got you."

"Not yet. I could only carry one rifle and crawl."

"What about the grenades?"

Carson grinned. "Right here in this bag, but I only found three."

"They'll have to do. Hand me the rifle. I'll give you cover fire, and you blow them to hell." Berg rose to one knee, braced the M-1 against his shoulder, and stood. His shots ricocheted off the rock, driving the soldiers down, and Carson threw the grenade, but it fell short. The explosion was loud, but harmless. "Harder, Max." Moe fired again. Carson grunted as he tossed the grenade, and, again, it came up short and blew up only dirt.

Raucous laughter sounded from behind the rock, and one of the German soldiers yelled, "My sister throws harder than that. Why don't you surrender?"

Berg handed the rifle to Carson. "Shit, we only have one left. Give it to me." He pulled the pin, held it close to his hip, and nodded for Carson to open fire. Then he shot up, shifted his feet, and threw it toward the rock like it was second base. A stunning blast, and there was silence.

"That's some fine throwing, Moe. Do you think they're dead?"

"If they're not, they're badly wounded. See if you can get this thing started, and I'll keep an eye on them." But, Moe couldn't leave it unsure. He sprinted to the rock, as Carson cranked the engine, and found both soldiers covered in blood. "They're done, Max." He walked back to the car and opened the truck. "This one's done too. Friendly fire." He pulled the body out, let it drop to the road, and said, "Let's get out of here, before we have more company. I'm ready to get out of this damn uniform."

"Me too, but what are you going to tell them about Galileo?"

"I think Martinez was lying through his teeth. If they're not working on the bomb project, they will be soon. Once the workers go home for the day, we need to bomb the shit out of it."

Chapter Nine

Moe,
Where are you? The weeks have turned into months, and
when you don't write, I worry. I hope you're not in Paris
with some floozy. I went to a party with Ethel at her
school. It was nice enough, but it reminded me of when we
went dancing. Well, I can't say what you did was really
dancing. Come home, my darling.
Stella

The remnants of what he'd seen in the camp hospital
tent, killing two men he didn't know, and another six
months of trying to convince Italian scientists to defect
left Moe Berg frustrated and exhausted. He had little time
to write Stella and, while their letters were always brief,
they grew increasingly so. His hotel room in Rome had
become a stately prison cell, holding him in a city he
wanted to leave and denying him the warmth and
companionship of the woman he loved so dearly. And,
now Treadwell came for a private meeting in this same
damned room.

"I'm leaving Rome soon, Moe."

"Did they fire you from the bakery? Too much yeast in
the bread?"

"I'm not the only one leaving. You're going too."

Berg couldn't restrain the smile that spread over his
face. "That's great news. It'll be good to have some time
at home. But, how soon will I be called back to the war?"

"No, you don't understand. You're not going home,
not yet. You're going behind enemy lines, in Poland."

"Poland? You can go to Poland, if you like. I'm going
home."

Treadwell seemed to ignore what he said. "We're going to drop you by parachute in a field in the northern part of Poland. A member of the Polish resistance will meet you at a farm house, and he'll tell you the rest."

"That's it? You're not going to tell me where the drop is or what I'm supposed to do when I get there or even who this guy is?"

"You will call him Kamil. You don't need to know more than that for now. You don't want to know more. Trust me on that. This is a matter of the most delicate nature. If you learn what we think you'll learn, then the Germans are going to have a tough time holding onto their allies, especially Italy."

Berg pushed his chair back and walked across the room to a table by the window. "Would you like some coffee, Mr. T?"

"No, thank you. Look, Moe, we don't normally try to explain things to our operatives. You get your orders and you follow them. That's how things work. But, in this case, I want you to know the importance of the mission. You may very well get yourself killed in Poland, and no one will ever know what happened to you."

"That's always a risk."

"It is, but this time the odds are stacked against you. If Kamil should be captured before you arrive or if you land in the wrong filed, you'll be stuck in hostile territory with no escape plan. Most of the time that means you die." Treadwell stood and kicked his chair over. "You know, I think I would like some of that coffee."

Moe poured another cup, calmly took it to Treadwell, and said, "I made it Irish."

"Well, that's good. I could use a drink." He raised the cup to take a sip and brought it back down. "My orders are to tell you nothing more than I have, but damn that. We estimate your chances of survival are in single-digit numbers, and you deserve to at least know where you're going."

"I understand the situation, Woodrow. Don't tell me anything that would get you into trouble."

"To hell with my getting into trouble. You're going to hell on earth – Auschwitz."

* * * *

Just a quick note, Stella. Now that I'm leaving, I can tell you I have been in Italy, and I will not be coming home soon. Don't be afraid but, if you don't hear from me, know how much I love you.
   Moe

The mystery of a night sky, the hum of a single-engine plane, and flashes of a strange country streaming past beneath him left Moe Berg somehow serene. He ran his hand down the tag line to his parachute and nodded, agreeing with himself, for the third time, that it was still there and still attached. The pilot spoke without turning. "We're approaching the drop zone. Our ground contacts tell us there's a moderate breeze out of the northwest, so be sure you jump exactly when I tell you to."

Moe pulled the door back and slid his feet to the edge of the opening. *All right, it's just like you practiced back in Maryland. Jump and float and touch down like landing on cotton. Yeah, cotton. Okay, I'm ready.* The pilot waved his arm, and Berg leapt into nothingness. He felt free for two seconds, before he felt a jerk. The round canopy billowed overhead, and he reached for two of the risers. He wondered why he even had risers, when he couldn't see where to steer himself. "Is that a flashlight? Yes, somebody's waving the crap out of it. Set her down, Moe, and then stop talking to yourself." His training showed him how difficult it was to control a parachute, but he couldn't worry about that now. He was falling and couldn't afford to miss the spot, but he did want to miss that tree. It seemed to grow taller as he neared it. He pulled his knees to his chest, as he sailed in. "Oh, shit!" His hip smacked a limb, putting him into a spin, and he hit the ground hard, his chute dragging him over the field.

When he stopped and came to his senses, a man stood over him with his light shining into Moe's eyes. "What is your name?" he asked.

"Romulus."

"I am Kamil." He helped Moe to his feet, and they carried the parachute into a barn. "We will bury this after you leave. For now, we must hide in case the Germans saw you."

"Saw me? It's dark as pitch out there."

"They have eyes everywhere. Bring your parachute and come with me." They walked to the back of the barn, and Kamil pushed a crate of rusty engine parts off an opening in the ground. "Take the ladder down to the hiding place, and I will follow." Moe loosed the harness of his parachute and dropped it into the hole. He descended into darkness, with only stray flashes from Kamil's light to guide the way. He felt a sense of dread, as Kamil pulled the crate back into place. "Stay where you are, and I will light the lantern. Yes, there, now we can see. Sit. We will talk, but keep your voice low and listen for any sounds above."

Berg dropped to the dirt floor. "Thank you for finding me, but let's cut to the chase. What am I doing here?"

Kamil stroked his full beard and sat beside Berg. "There is a Nazi prison camp about sixty kilometers from this spot, the Auschwitz camp at Brzezinka. It is called

Birkenau. We have heard for months about what happens there. We have watched trains arrive filled with prisoners almost every day, but the trains always leave empty."

"Why would that be unusual? Prisoners of war aren't generally released until the war is over or someone makes a trade for them."

"You don't understand. The trains bring thousands of people every week, many of them women and children, not just soldiers. They have brought more than a hundred thousand this month. The people of the towns around the prison complain of an odor they can't explain."

"Is it sewage? I mean, when you put that many people together, it's like a city, and the crap's got to go somewhere."

"The people say they've never smelled this odor before, but I have smelled it. It is the smell of burning flesh."

"Bull shit. I've heard the rumors about the Nazis and their death squads, but they're just that, rumors. We don't live in the Middle Ages. There are rules of war. Even Hitler must have some sense of decency."

"You do not believe me, but you will when you see it." He took a folder from the corner of the room and handed it to Berg. "These are your papers."

Moe opened the folder and leafed through its pages under the light of the lantern. "What's this?"

"That is your agreement to never discuss what you see inside the prison, under penalty of death. You must sign it to gain entry."

"These guys take security seriously. And, my name is Oleg Nowack from Warsaw. My father and I have been supplying the camp with vegetables for the past year, and I'm on my way to renegotiate the contract." He read the rest of the description quietly and lit the corner of the paper with the flame of the lantern.

"Don't you want to keep that and study it?"

"I don't need to read it more than once. I'm not worried about remembering who I am, but I am a little worried about Oleg Nowack. I assume he's a real person. Do they know him at this camp?"

"We don't think so. He is arriving in Gdansk tomorrow by train. Our contacts in Warsaw say the father is aging and wants his son to run the business. This trip is meant for him to meet the commandant and sign an extension to the contract."

"And, exactly who is this commandant?"

"His name is Rudolf Hoss, and he is Satan on earth. He is a charming and cruel man. You will find his dossier in the back of your folder. Colonel Hoss is in charge of all the Auschwitz prisons, and he makes the trip to Birkenau for a day or two each week."

"How do you plan to get the real Nowack out of the way, so I can replace him?"

"You don't need to know that."

"The hell I don't. You want me to walk into a Nazi prisoner-of-war camp, not knowing whether they will immediately know I am a fraud, and without some assurance that the real guy won't walk in right behind me. That scenario doesn't work for me. You tell me or I walk out."

"Then you must walk out. You will find it difficult to escape the Nazi patrols without our help, but you are very welcome to try."

"Have it your way." Berg laid the folder on the floor, passed by Kamil, and climbed to the top of the ladder.

"Wait. Nowack will hire a car at the train station and take the road from Gdensk to the camp. We have identified a place where we can intercept the car and kidnap him or, if necessary, kill him."

Moe stepped back down and sat on the floor again. "No, no, no. I can't show up in a car with bullet holes in it, and what about the driver? Are you going to kill him too?"

"If it becomes necessary."

"When we start killing innocent people, how are we different from the Nazis? I won't be part of that. Now, you listen to me. Have a man, carrying a sign with Nowack's name, waiting on the platform when he arrives. Tell him Colonel Hoss sent the car to bring him to the camp, kind of a gesture of friendship. But, the driver will be one of our people. He drives Nowack to a secluded place where we take him, no muss, no fuss."

"That could work. We will blindfold Nowack and release him once you've left the country. Is that kind enough for you?"

"It's not as much about being kind as it is about being smart. I've tried to pass myself off as a major twice, and they found me out both times. If Colonel Hoss really is murdering people in that camp, I don't want to be his next victim."

* * * *

Berg rode in the back seat wearing a brown suit, white shirt, and Oleg Nowack's signature polka-dot bowtie. He'd never been to Poland before, and it was not his strongest language. Would he have the right inflections in his voice? Would he demonstrate the mannerisms of a Pole? The car exited a copse of trees, and Auschwitz Birkenau came into view. The entry gate centered a long, red-brick building with a guard tower overhead. Two rows of electrified fencing surrounded an enormous campus. "My God, that place must be fifteen or twenty-thousand acres." he whispered. And, the odor was unmistakable. It reminded him of the field hospital he visited, only worse, much worse. They stopped at the security building and waited as they searched the car, and then drove to the commandant's office. Berg stepped out carrying Nowack's valise with three bottles of wine inside. He paused by the driver's window and said, "Stay here. Have a smoke if you like. I don't expect to be in there very long."

His gaze ran down the rows of buildings on each side of the railway tracks. *I wish I'd brought my Bell and Howell.* He entered the door still wondering whether he would be alive in ten minutes. The soldier at the desk offered to take the valise, but Berg said, "No, thank you. I have samples for the colonel." His heart beat rose, as the solder escorted him into the commandant's private office. *Oh, boy, here it comes. Look at his eyes, Moe, and get ready to run. Huh, run where?*

Hoss signed something, handed a stack of papers to the soldier, and dismissed him. And, he turned to Moe. "Ah, so you are Albert's son, Oleg."

"Yes, Colonel, and it is my pleasure to meet you at last. My father speaks of you with respect and affection."

"That is good to hear. We have done business together for some time, ever since my arrival here. Did you bring the secrecy agreement?" Berg pulled it from the valise, followed by the bottles of wine. "I see your father taught you the value of friendship. You may put those on my desk. And, please have a seat so we may talk."

Berg set the wine down and took a seat in a wooden, ladder-back chair. He watched the trim, forty-two-year-old study the form, as he took his seat, and shoved it into a desk drawer. "My father said he sent you a copy of the contracts last week. Did they arrive safely?"

"They arrived, and I have studied them thoroughly. Your prices are fair, but we may be adding additional troops soon, perhaps two hundred. We will pay you a good price. You see, we are not Communists. Can you provide more food if we need it?"

"We can. It would be helpful to have two weeks' notice to make those arrangements. I assume those additional troops will also mean more prisoners? Do you have an estimate of how much food you will need for them? As you know, meat products are difficult to find."

"The prisoners don't need meat. They have soup for lunch and bread for dinner. They are animals and deserve no better. Ah, yes, this is your first visit. You don't know how the camp works, do you? I must remedy that. Come. I will give you a quick tour of the facility, and you will better understand our needs."

"I don't want to impose on you, Commandant, but, if you have the time, that would be very helpful."

"It is no trouble at all. In fact, for the son of my friend, I must insist that you join my family and me for lunch." He raised his hand. "No, no, I will not accept your refusal. Protocol demands it."

"You are most kind. It would be my honor to meet your family."

They stood, walked out of the building, and stopped on the narrow stoop. A thin smile crept over Hoss' face, and he said, "You will be seeing things most people will never see. And, you understand that, if you should disclose these things, we will shoot you?" Berg nodded, and Hoss laughed aloud. He pulled his cap over his short hair, called for his car, and described the camp, as they drove beside the railroad tracks. "The camp is divided into sections. Over there are women's barracks. They were designed to house seven-hundred-fifty, but we are more efficient than

162

the designers. Each of our barracks can accommodate one thousand."

"I can see why efficiency would be important. You must have a hundred barracks or more."

"That is where we keep the Gypsies. We segregate the population by ancestry and gender. I'm sure you understand that we must manage the carnal nature of these people. If we let the men and women interact, we would be overrun with their bastard children. They have no morals."

"The uniforms are all black-and-white stripes. How do you keep track of who the prisoners are or what race they are?"

"An excellent question, Oleg. Each prisoner is assigned a number, and those numbers are tattooed onto their left arms. You can see they all have a triangle stitched to the front of the uniform. For example, the Jews have yellow triangles, and purple is for Jehovah's Witnesses."

"I understand the Jews. They are a blight on mankind, but what crime have the Jehovah's Witnesses committed?
"

"They refuse to support the Reich, or any government for that matter. They will not go to war and they will not salute a national flag. Their crime is treason. Come, I will show you what happens to traitors." They rode to the end of the women's camp and stopped near a building with concrete walls. "This is where we dispose of the undesirables. We tell them it is a shower house. We even have a room for them to undress before they bathe. It helps control them, so they don't riot."

"Those drums behind that corner. Is that Zyklon B, the pesticide?"

"I am impressed, Oleg, that you recognize it so quickly, but it has a use beyond being a pesticide. We receive it in capsule form from the IG Farben chemical plant in Monowitz. When the capsule is dropped into a container of acid, we have cyanide gas. It is the most compassionate and efficient way to dispose of people, and we don't waste bullets. We have four gas chambers in operation. I can exterminate ten thousand in a single day. Of course, the problem isn't killing them. It's handling the bodies after. But then, that's why we have cremation ovens." Again, Hoss grinned. "Does it make you queasy to hear these things?"

"Perhaps a bit. I am a merchant, the freshest produce in all of Poland."

"Then, let us move on before you lose your appetite. Driver, to my home." They rolled past nondescript buildings on both sides and a large crematorium before exiting through a gate in the north fence. "Perhaps this area will suit you better, Oleg. Most of our guards live here with their wives and children, just as I do. To the left is the theatre and just there the swimming pool."

"And, what of that shop?"

"It is our coffee house. The soldiers don't use it so much as their wives do. It gives them a place to meet, drink a coffee, and share the news of the day. Local merchants visit twice per week to show the latest fashions and take orders for kitchenware, toys for the children, and the like. We can't provide everything they would have in Germany, but we try to accommodate their needs as we can."

"I must say you have done well by your people. They live better than the people in Warsaw."

"And, they should. These men sacrifice everything for the Fatherland. I want them to know the Fuerher appreciates what they do. When the war is over, they will all be rewarded for their service. Think of it, Oleg, a world

164

without disease-laden scum." He squeezed Berg's knee. "Forgive me. I sometimes get emotional thinking about how the world can be, and how it will be. Our children and grandchildren will be able to attend the finest schools without being held back by primates, like Jews and Gypsies. Can you imagine the progress we will make in medicine and science, when the brightest minds take their rightful place? I tell you it excites me."

"Is that your home?"

"Yes, it was built especially for my family. My wife loves the outdoors, so I had it placed on the hillside facing away from the camp. She deserves a view that is not marred by the vermin in the camp." The car stopped by the front steps, and Hoss escorted Berg inside. "Hedwig, come and meet our guest."

A plain-looking woman with brown hair and dressed in white came out of the kitchen to the living room. "Good morning, sir. Welcome to our home."

Berg kissed her hand and said, "It is a great pleasure to meet you, Mrs. Hoss. By your dress, I take it you are a nurse."

"Yes, and I'm afraid I must be very rude and leave you." She turned to Hoss. "Rudolf, one of the soldiers was injured, and I must go to him."

"Is it a serious injury, my dear?"

"A laceration on his arm, but Dr. Mengele asked that I assist him. He doesn't trust the other nurses."

"Of course, and where are the children?'

"Ingebright, Klaus, and Hans are at the library, and my mother is looking after Heidetraut and the baby in the guest house." She kissed his cheek, smiled at Berg, and hurried out the door.

Hoss called after her, laughing. "Tell Dr. Mengele the man is a soldier, and he is not to experiment on him."

Berg forced a smile onto his face. "Excuse my little joke. I suppose we are left to lunch at the coffee shop."

"Your wife is lovely, Colonel, and I appreciate so much your invitation to lunch, but perhaps I should go now. I do have a train to catch, and I would like to get back to town before dark. The roads are filled with highwaymen."

"Oh, I had hoped to get to know you much better, but, as your host, I will yield to your wishes. I will accompany you back to my office."

They returned to the car, drove back inside the fence, and followed the railroad tracks. "Let me thank you again for your kindness to me, and I can promise you we will do our very best to meet your every need." His voice trailed off under the sound of a train approaching. It stopped thirty feet from Hoss' office. Armed soldiers surrounded the boxcars, as men, women, and children lowered themselves to the ground. Berg watched quietly, as the guards arranged them into a long line. A German captain stood at the head of the line, directing some to the left and others to the right, as they filed past him. "I thought you separated the men from the women."

"That comes later for the ones he sends to the right. Those the captain determines not to be suitable for labor are sent to the left. As we say here, 'To the right is life.' The rest are sent to the showers."

"And, the children? Do you exterminate them?"

"We keep the ones who are old enough and strong enough to work. The others are of no use to us. We've tried keeping them, but they inevitably get typhus and die anyway." Berg watched a young girl, holding her mother's hand as they were funneled to the gas chamber. He wanted to grab a rifle and shoot Hoss on the spot, but it would not save any lives. Perhaps surviving this, and getting back to his people, could. He felt the commandant's hand settle onto his shoulder and heard his voice. "Don't worry, Oleg. You won't have to bring us baby food."

* * * *

Moe managed to keep his anger buried inside and left Auschwitz with signed contracts in his valise. When the car was safely back in the cover of trees, he screamed and cursed until his throat was sore and his voice nearly gone. The good news was that no motorcycles were chasing them, but he got the bad news when he reached Kamil at the farmhouse. "I am sorry to tell you this, my friend, but somehow Oleg Nowack managed to escape."

"What? You know he'll go straight to the prison camp. How could this happen?"

"I do not know. I left two men to guard him, but he got free of his bindings and disappeared."

"Yeah, well, Rudolf Hoss is going to make me disappear, if he finds me. Okay, okay, we can't undo what is done. The prison is everything you thought it was and more. It's more important than ever that I get back alive. The Allies need to know how brutal the Nazis really are, and I'm the one to tell them."

"We've tried to tell them before, but they would not listen."

"That's why I kept the contracts. They have Hoss's signature, and that proves I was inside. Now, what's the extraction plan?"

"We will take you by truck to Leba, and there we have a boat. Once you are in Denmark, you must find your way home. But, we must wait for nightfall to leave."

"Does that mean I go back into your private room in the barn?"

"It does."

"Well, that's just perfect. Open the trunk, will you? I stashed a bottle of wine in there. If I'm going to be stuck in a hole for five or six hours, I might as well have a drink. After what I saw today, I think I need the whole bottle. But, before you sink me in the ground again, I need the radio from my sack." Kamil raked dirt off a green bag with the tip of a shovel, pulled a radio from inside, and handed it to Berg. "Thank you." He held it to his face and said, "Honey Pie, this is Joker. Come in. Honey Pie, this is Joker, Come in."

A woman's voice answered through the static. "Joker, this is Honey Pie. Go ahead."

"Honey Pie, this is Joker. Need a taxi, repeat, need a taxi. Location Harvey, tomorrow at purple hour."

"We read you, Joker. Tomorrow, location Harvey, purple hour. Confirm."

"That is confirmed, Honey Pie. Thank you and out." Berg handed the radio back to Kamil and smiled. "Don't mind us. That's my sweetheart, and we talk like that all the time."

* * * *

The lantern flame flickered, and the air seemed thinner than when Berg entered the hole in the barn. As the hours crawled by, he drained the bottle of wine and tossed it aside. Where was Kamil? Had the Nazis captured him? He heard the sound of someone dragging the crate off the opening and wondered if it might be German soldiers. And, he knew the feeling of being vulnerable, not even a pistol to defend himself. A voice called from above. "Don't come out yet." A package fell down the ladder. "Put these clothes on and then come up."

Berg tore the package open to find a leather jacket, shirt, and trousers, all black. He changed as quickly as he could and hurried up the ladder. Fresh air and the sight of open fields brought him back to life. "The next time I need to hide, Kamil, let's find something better than a blasted hole in the ground."

"It is the best we have for now, and be glad you were there. We have seen Nazi patrols pass by three times."

"Yeah, I imagine they're hot for me. Well, I guess we should be going, but first I need a gun."

"Guns are difficult to come by and ammunition is just as scarce. Our people need the weapons they have. We cannot give you what we don't have."

"Don't give me that line. I know you've killed at least one German soldier in the past week. You know how important it is for me to get back safely, so hand it over. I'll give it back once I'm on the boat."

Kamil paused and said, "They told me you would be a difficult man to deal with." He pulled a Luger from his coat pocket. "Here, take this, but we have only the bullets that are in the clip. You must use them wisely."

"I will. Thank you." They left the barn and walked to a battered horse truck with a man stationed on each side, holding baskets of apples. "Is this my ride out of here?"

"Do you need to relieve yourself before we leave?"

"I took care of that in the hole."

"Good. Then climb into the box in the back of the truck and lay down in the box."

Berg pulled himself up, grumbling as he rose. "Damn, the things I do for my country." He lay flat in the wooden crate, and the men poured their apples over him. "Take it easy, guys. We don't want to bruise the fruit." No one laughed, and Berg was only glib in hopes of calming his nerves. The people of Auschwitz preyed on his mind, as the truck rocked into motion. How many more would die tomorrow and the next day and the next, before he could reach London and tell his story? He remembered Colonel

Hoss' joke about Dr. Mengele not experimenting on his wounded soldier. What if he were caught? Would they experiment on him before killing him?

The truck jostled through the night, and he had no sense of where it was going. All he could see between the apples was the tarp that covered the truck bed. It was grave-like, but with the fragrance of apples instead of dirt. He couldn't ask for much more than for the truck to keep moving. As long as it was moving, there was hope. And, then it stopped. Berg listened, as Kamil spoke in broken German. "We are but farmers, travelling to Lebork to sell our wares."

"Then why do you travel so late into the night?" a voice asked.

"The road is narrow and it is crowded during the day. And, we wish to have our apples ready to sell when the market opens."

"If this is true, you don't need to travel to the market. We are but three kilometers from the Lauenberg camp. The commandant would buy your apples, if they are good enough for his soldiers. Come, let me see them."

"We have had a poor season. My fruit is small and worm ridden. I fear it is not suitable for the commandant's men."

The soldier's voice grew stern. "Show me your apples."

Berg listened to the sound of a metallic click. *Bayonet. Oh, shit, he's in the truck*. The beam of a flashlight swept over the crate, and Berg saw bits of the soldier's face and his bayonet.

"These apples look fine to me."

He raised his rifle to thrust the blade through the apples, and Berg shot him in the head. Another shot rose from outside the truck, and then another. Berg sat up with fruit spilling from the crate to the truck bed. He pointed his gun toward the back of the tailgate, and a dark figure stepped into his sights, his pistol pointed at Berg. "Kamil?"

"He did not kill you? Good, then let us not shoot each other." He shoved his gun under his belt. "Come. We will move the bodies out of sight."

Berg rolled out of the box and dropped off the back of the truck. He pulled one body into a ditch, while Kamil dragged the other behind a row of trees. "I wonder whether anyone heard the shots."

"Perhaps, and we must be on our way. Get into the box, and I will cover you with the apples again."

"No. We'll gather up the spilled apples, but I'm riding with you the rest of the way. If they stop us, I'll be your cousin. That would be easier to sell than trying to explain why I'm hiding in a crate of apples."

"If you wish, but we must hurry."

"How far are we from Leba?"

"It is but thirty kilometers from here. We can reach it in an hour, if we are not stopped again."

"Then, let's get at it. I've killed enough people lately. It's beginning to wear on me." Berg rode with his hand on the gun in his pocket, watching every bush and turn in the road, and wishing the night would be over.

* * * *

A spray of sunlight glistened on the waters of the Baltic Sea. Berg walked to the edge of the water and stepped into a rubber raft. "My God, this is beautiful. It almost makes you forger we're at war."

"But, we are at war, my friend." Kamil answered. "And, I will leave you here. The raft will take you to a steamboat waiting around that shoal, and the boat will take you to Denmark. But, beware of Nazi gunboats. It is a long and dangerous trip."

"Don't worry too much about that. I've made arrangements."

Kamil's bearded face turned a snide grin. "I would be surprised if you had not. Good luck, and God's speed."

Berg didn't speak to the man rowing the raft, and he spoke little to the crew on the steamboat. They sailed northwest for two hours and twelve minutes, and Berg asked the captain to stop. "But, we cannot stop here. Every wasted minute puts my crew at risk of capture. We should have sailed at night."

"I'm afraid I'm the one who asked that you set sail during daylight hours." He pointed over the port side of the boat. "Do you see that dot out there?"

The captain raised binoculars to his eyes. "I see a periscope. You have brought us to a German u boat, and they will sink us. We will all die."

"We will all die, Captain, but not today." The dot rose from the waters, and the top of a submarine appeared with the image of a British flag painted on its conn tower. "Would you please lower the raft? That's my ride, and she's right on time, exactly purple hour."

* * * *

"What do you mean they won't move on Auschwitz? I'll bet they've murdered a million people in that place, some of them kids."

Treadwell took a cigarette from a box on his desk, lit it, and said, "Look, Moe, I've taken your story to everyone I know. There isn't an American official in London who hasn't heard me beg them to invade. Hell, I went to the Prime Minister's office, and they all say the same thing."

"Yes, I know. We need our troops at the front. If we liberate the prisoners, then we have to take care of them, and that takes more troops. I've heard it a dozen times. They could at least bomb Hoss' office building and kill that son of a bitch."

"And, the Nazis would replace him within a week."

Berg paced across the room, mumbling with each breath, and stared out the window at Big Ben. "If they won't listen, we'll go to the President."

"Be serious. Just how do you expect to get access to President Roosevelt?"

"Nelson Rockefeller is his friend, and I worked for him in South America for nearly two years. He owes me."

Treadwell lifted the telephone receiver. "Here, dial zero and ask for the international operator." He held the receiver for a long moment and set it back on the cradle. "You're just going to have to wait."

"Shit."

"And, that's not all, Moe. I got word on your friend Eiji Sawamura. He's dead."

"Oh, God. Eiji was just a kid. I bet he wasn't over twenty-two or twenty-three. What happened?"

"Details are a little sketchy, but he was on a ship we sank near Yakushima. We heard about it through Japanese radio. He was their hero."

"Mine too. He was the most dedicated young man I ever met. The sad part is he gave his life for an Emperor who didn't give a damn about him. What a shame. It breaks my heart."

* * * *

Chancellor's Pub was quiet on this Wednesday evening, and Moe sat at the bar with his third glass of dark ale. He couldn't forget the image of that little girl, marching to her death. It haunted his waking hours and punished him with nightmares at day's end. *Damn the*

Army. Damn the Air Force. Damn the politics that make people turn their backs until it's convenient to look. He hardly noticed the gray skirt that slid onto the stool beside him.

"Hello, baseball man," she said.

"Well, I'll be damned. Lydia Farmington, my favorite MI6 agent. I see you survived Brazil."

"Barely. I thought they might get me when Admiral Canaris was arrested, but here I am, still alive. And, what about you, Moe Berg? Where have you been these many months?"

"Oh, you know, here and there."

"Are you still handing out condoms to your soldiers and teaching them the curve ball?"

"You know, I never could throw a curve, not on purpose. Sometimes, I'd try to throw a runner out, and the ball would slice one way of the other, but I couldn't figure out how to replicate that. If I could have, I might have made some real money pitching."

"Do you have enough money to buy me a drink?"

"Sure. Bartender, bring the lady whatever she wants." She nodded, and the bartender went to work on a mixed drink. "You must be a regular, or is this guy one of your people posing as a bartender?"

"If he is, he makes a good whiskey sour, and that's all I care about."

"I can't speak for whiskey sour, but the ale is good, room temperature, but still good." He held his drink in front of his face and said, "Oh little glass of mighty power, charmer of an idle hour, object of my warm desire." He set the glass down. "I'm afraid I have misquoted

Lord Byron's poem, but it just seemed appropriate today."

Her drink arrived, and she swilled it in one long gulp. "Damn, that is some serious drinking."

"I like a good drink, and I seem to be growing fonder of hard liquor. I have more at my flat. Would you like to come over for a drink or six or ten? I wouldn't mind a little diversion tonight."

The effects of the alcohol ran through his mind and down his body, triggering his most primal desires. "Now, that is an intriguing invitation. I've never had sex with a black woman, but you are the most beautiful thing I've seen in a year. And, I bet you could make a man forget what's troubling him."

She dropped her hand onto his thigh. "I can do a lot more than that." She stood and took his hand. "Come on, Moe. In our business, there are no guarantees, not even another breath. We have to grab life when we can, and I don't let the rule makers in polite society decide what I'm going to do."

He sat for a moment with every part of his body aglow. He pulled her hand to his lips, kissed it, and said, "I want you so bad I can taste it, and I mean that literally. I can't think of anything I'd rather do tonight than wrap you around me and make love till next Thursday, but I've got a girl at home, and she deserves better than to have me cheat on her."

"She'll never know. You can trust me on that."

"But, I'll know, and that's enough." He released her hand and laid some money on the bar. "It's time for Moe Berg to go home." But, his exit from the bar, and from England, was delayed by the scream of an air raid siren. "Oh, boy, that can't be good."

Lydia grabbed his hand, as the bartender turned out the lights and locked the door. "Hurry," she said. "To the cellar." She pulled the big man behind the bar and through a narrow opening to a set of stairs. They clattered down the concrete steps, followed by two other patrons and the bartender. The heavy door slammed shut like the gate of a prison cell. She tugged on his arm, dragging him to a bench by the earthen wall. The glow of candlelight shone on her smooth skin, as she studied his face. "Is this your first time to be bombed, Moe?"

"In the literal sense, yes. I take it this isn't your first time."

"It feels like they bomb us every night, but I only got back to London six months ago, so I haven't seen as much of it as most people. Try to relax. It shouldn't last more than half an hour, and we can go back up, assuming they don't kill us."

"Well, that's encouraging. You have a way of making me feel so much better about our situation." The first bomb hit, followed by three more, and the room shook, clods of dirt falling from the walls. "Whoa, that was close."

"Not really. You'll know when it gets close." She pulled his arm around her shoulders. "I'm sorry about this, Moe, but these bombings scare the life out of me. Do you mind?"

He rubbed her shoulder and pulled her head to his chest. "To tell the truth, they scare me a little bit too. We'll just hold onto each other, and maybe we can ride this thing out." It had been a long time since he held a woman, other than Stella, in his arms. Somehow things didn't seem quite as dire under the scent of her perfume. *My God*, he thought. *How many times do I have to hide in a hole in the ground?* He imagined the night skies were filled with thunder, a cloudburst no one had predicted. After all, that's why they carried so many umbrellas in

176

England. This was nothing more, and yet the thunder was all around them and growing closer. A sudden blast knocked them from the bench and into darkness.

Berg hit the floor hard. For a moment he wasn't sure if he was alive or dead. When he came to his senses, he reached for her. "Lydia? Are you there?" She didn't answer. "Lydia!" The flash of a match broke through the darkness, as the bartender lit a candle. And, there she lay, blood oozing from the side of her head. Moe pulled her up and patted her face, but she didn't move. He pressed his handkerchief over the wound and called to the bartender. "Do you have bandages?"

"Not down here."

"Where are they?"

"Are you crazy? They're still bombing us."

"Damn it, man. Where are they?"

"In a drawer under the till, but you'll both die, if you go up there."

He lifted her into his arms, yanked the door open, and scampered up the stairs. Broken glass covered the barroom floor, and the door the bartender had taken such care to lock was blown off its hinges. Moe held her against his side with one arm, brushed debris from the bar with the other, and laid her limb body on the polished mahogany. He fashioned a compress and wrapped her head with gauze. As he doused a cloth with ammonia, a block buster hit down the street, knocking him to his knees and shattering the mirror behind him. "German bastards!" He pulled himself up, worried that Lydia had been hurt even worse, but she lay unharmed. The odor of ammonia under her nose brought a cough and a frown. "That's my girl. You're too stubborn to die."

She smiled and said, "You could at least buy me a drink before you try to poison me."

"I'll do that, but first let's get back downstairs. I don't think they're through with us." He carried her back down the narrow steps, as the Luftwaffe started its second deadly pass over the city.

Chapter Ten

Berg left the overcast skies of London behind him and came home, without specific orders telling him could. He called the OSS office from the airport in Washington and took the train for New York, the train to Stella. He had ridden in this same club car many times, and yet this trip seemed so long, so slow. *Open this thing up, man. Stop dragging your ass*. But, in time he reached Grand Central Station. He left the train with a single suitcase and took quick steps toward the terminal, looking for Stella with every stride. And, he dropped his suitcase when he saw her, standing by a large window, silhouetted in the sunlight. She ran for his open arms. "Moe, Moe. Thank God you're home."

Moe held her close, her tears wetting the side of his neck. He was home. He was finally with the woman he loved, but where was the Justice of the Peace? It didn't matter now. Their kisses were free of desire, but filled with compassion and hope and a burning devotion for each other. They locked arms and walked to the car. He took her hand as she drove down Madison Avenue. "I'm not going back, Stell."

"What do you mean? You're not going back to Europe?"

"I'm not going back to the OSS. I've done enough. I quit."

"Well, that's fine with me."

"I'll talk to the Yankees and see if they can use me as a coach. Hell, worst case scenario, I'll settle for being a lawyer, but I'm through with war. I'm through with the lying and killing and everything that goes with it."

"You don't know how happy that makes me."

"Yeah, me too. We're going to settle down in the Big Apple and have a life together, a real life. This time I'm home to stay."

* * * *

A week passed, then two, and Berg couldn't stand another day of listening to music students plunking on Stella's piano. He took the subway across town, a bus to Newark, and a taxi to his mother's house. They finished lunch, and he washed the dishes, while his mother read the newspaper on the sofa. "Why don't you open the curtains, Mama? You'll ruin your eyes in there."

"I'm fine. I have the lamp. That's enough. Did you talk to the people with the Yankees?"

"Yes. I saw Joe McCarthy, but he said they're fixed for coaches for this season. He said he'd keep me in mind for next year, if somebody moves on." He dried his hands, walked to the window, and pulled back the drapes. "There. Let's get some sunlight in here. The house is so dreary when you keep it closed up like that."

"I suppose you're right, but I don't seem to have much energy since your father died. Sam went off to California, Ethel has her own life now, and you've been gone so long. There doesn't seem to be much reason for me to do much anymore."

He sat beside her and kissed her cheek. "Don't talk like that. I'm home now, and Ethel comes by on weekends, doesn't she?"

"That's all she does and, with all the time she spends away, you'd think she'd have a man by now." She pressed a finger into his chest. "And, what about you, Moe? When are you going to marry that sweet girl?"

"It's funny you should ask. I've been wondering that myself."

"Is something wrong, son? Did you find another girl over there in Europe?"

"No, it's nothing like that. Stella is still my girl, but something is different. I don't know exactly what, but, well, maybe it's me. I'm not the same man I was when I left here. Mama, I saw people treated in ways I never would've believed, if I hadn't seen it for myself. And, I'm still not sure it wasn't all a bad dream, a very bad dream."

"You always were the sensitive one. I remember when you were six years old and brought home that scrawny cat."

"No, Mama, it isn't that. I've changed and I wonder if Stella still wants a man who's gone through those kinds of changes."

"Don't worry about Stella. She loves you. You should get out of that apartment. Take her somewhere, maybe the theatre or a nice restaurant."

"Well, that's an idea. Maybe I could take her back to Lindy's. We went there on our first date."

"Ethel said she likes that place; although, I don't know why. It's full of gangsters."

"Gangsters have to eat too, Mama. So, how does Ethel know that?"

"Oh, she's been keeping track of Stella while you were gone. They went to the movies and dinner, not at Lindy's of course. Ethel couldn't afford that, but Stella told her she'd been going there with friends."

"But, I know all her friends and, well, it doesn't matter. Lindy's it is. I'll call for reservations and take her tonight." He patted his mother's hand and stood. "I should be going, if I'm to make it home in time to take Stella to dinner. They don't hold the busses, not even for old baseball players."

* * * *

Neon lights gleamed onto the wet streets outside 1626 Broadway, painting the street in hues of blue and red. Moe paid the cab driver, took Stella's hand, and they walked under the sign that flashed one word - *Lindy's*. The maître d took them to a table in the corner, and Moe ordered a bottle of wine. "Do you remember this place, Stell?"

"I should. That was a strange night, coming here with some baseball player who called me out of the blue. I never thought I'd do that. It was so out of character for me." Her voice softened. "But, I'm glad I did." They sat quietly, talking only with their hearts, and the wine arrived. Stella scanned the room, as the waiter poured. "Moe, is that Milton Berle?"

"He comes here almost every night. I think it's a Jewish thing, or maybe he likes the food."

"Look at the guy in the corner. I didn't know men wore spats anymore."

"Don't look too closely. That's Arnold Rothstein, the guy who rigged the World Series a few years ago, and he has all those body guards for a reason. He's the head of the Jewish Mafia, and he'd as soon kill you as comb his hair."

"If he's so bad, how do you know him?"

"He sent a couple of his goons to see me about fixing a game, when I played for the Red Sox. It's hard to say no to a guy like that, especially when they mention your family by name. So, I told them I was just a backup catcher, I probably wouldn't even play that night, so I wouldn't be of any help to them. When I got to the park, I faked an ankle strain to make sure I didn't get into the game."

"I'm glad you don't have to worry about that kind of thing now."

The waiter set the bottle aside and said, "It's so good to see you again, Miss Huni. What may I get for you this evening?"

"I'll have the roast chicken with asparagus and creamed potatoes."

"And, you sir?"

"I'll have the same." Moe waited for the waiter to leave and said, "How is it that he knows your name?"

She lowered her gaze for a moment and then looked into his eyes. "I was terribly lonely while you were gone, Moe. For the first few months, I sat home, feeling sorry for myself. I was miserable, just miserable."

"But, I thought Ethel was going places with you."

"She was, and that helped. In fact, I brought her here one night to say thank you. We had dinner and cocktails, and I saw some people I knew at another table, Tom and Susan Fredericks. They stopped to speak on their way out and, well, they introduced me to their friend, a naval officer named Charles Atkins."

"Oh? Did you …"

"No. I did not sleep with him. We became good friends, and we had dinner a few times, but that was all. He was a shoulder to lean on while you were gone, but I was always faithful to you. I love you, Moe."

He turned a crooked grin. "Did he ask you to marry him?"

"Three times, and I said no every time."

"Is that why things have been so cool between us? Has something changed?"

"It's been stressful. I wanted you to come home so badly and, now that you're here, I guess I'm not sure what I should do with you. It's like asking for a pony for Christmas and, for some crazy reason, your parents buy one, and what do you do with a pony in New York?"

183

"I'm not sure what that means, but I'll take it for what it's worth. You made a friend, who happened to be a guy, and now we're together again. I'll stay with you this time, and you won't need another friend."

"That's all I want, Moe, for you to be home with me. It's the way it should be."

* * * *

Rosie the Riveter was busy building planes and tanks for the war effort, but Moe Berg was still looking for a job. Working in sports and espionage had not built the kind of resume that most law firms were looking for. So, he walked the streets, following up with the hiring managers who had told him "maybe later", and he ended each day seated on a bench near the docks, watching tankers and tugboats sailing by. Each day stripped a little more of his manhood, his self-confidence, his sense of who he was.

His lunch lay heavy in his stomach early on a Friday afternoon. Not even the newspaper spread over his lap could break his aimless stare. But, a man beside him on the bench did. "Hey, buddy. You better grab that paper before you lose it."

"What? Oh, I'm sorry. I didn't see you sit down."

He stroked his rotund belly and answered with a strong Brooklyn accent. "Not too many miss a big guy like me. You must be a little out of you head, huh?"

"I suppose I am, but I didn't mean to ignore you."

"Forget about it. It don't matter. I just pulled over to grab a smoke before my next fare."

"You drive a taxi?"

"You better believe it. Best hack in the city. Just ask anybody. Hey, you're sitting in Manhattan, right?"

"Yes, more or less."

"You want to get from her to Queens? I'm your guy. You want cross to over to Jersey? I'll get you there before you can finish that newspaper. There ain't nobody can work the back streets of New York like me. Rocco Hines, he's the best. Uh, that's me, Rocco Hines." He paused to light his cigarette, spewed a cloud of smoke, and spit a fragment of tobacco from his tongue. "So, uh, what about you, pal? What's your gig?"

Moe folded the paper and started to spin one of his yarns, but somehow he didn't quite have the energy to muster a good lie. "Well, right now, my gig is sitting on park benches."

"Oh, that's tough. It's no good being out of a job. Did you think about joining the Army?"

"I considered it, but I'm a little on the mature side for that. They seem to prefer younger guys."

"What's your background? If you know the city and can drive like a maniac, I could put a word in for you at dispatch."

"That's very kind of you, Rocco, but I'm afraid I don't drive. My jobs have been unconventional."

"Yeah? You ain't some kind of street peddler, are you?"

"No, it isn't that. Do you like baseball, Rocco?"

"Shit, who don't. I mean, hey, I thought you looked familiar. I think I saw your picture one time, but I can't remember the name."

"It's Berg, Moe Berg."

"Yeah, you played for the Red Sox."

"The Red Sox, the Senators, White Sox, and a few more. I guess I made the circuit."

"Did you ever play against the Babe?"

"Oh, yes, we even traveled to Japan together. I played the Babe, Gehrig, Cobb, all the big names."

"Ty Cobb? You played against Ty Cobb? Bullshit. You're bullshitting me."

"It's true, Rocco. He was the best I ever saw, but what an asshole."

"Well, I'll be damned. You used to be somebody important, didn't you?"

Moe raised a sad smile. "Yes, I suppose I was, but it seems like a long time ago. "

Hines crushed his cigarette butt under his shoe and stood to go. "Well, it was good to meet you, Moe. The wife won't believe it when I tell I met somebody who played with Babe Ruth."

"Would she believe you gave that guy a ride to his apartment?"

"Oh, you need to get home? Hell, I'm you man. Come on, but we need to hurry. I'm parked in a tow zone."

Berg followed him to his cab and enjoyed a relatively quiet ride to the front of the apartment building. He paid the fare, included a generous tip, and crossed the sidewalk. The doorman nodded, as Moe entered the building and stopped to pick up the mail before taking the elevator to Stella's apartment. "What this? A letter for me? God, I hope it's a job offer." He tore the envelop open as he entered the door, and Stella greeted him with a quick kiss.

"Any luck today?" she asked.

"Not yet. I was hoping this letter might be something, but it's a ticket."

"A ticket? Who's it from?"

"I don't know. It's a round-trip fare from Grand Central to Boston and back. The train leaves in the morning. Here, look. Maybe you can make something out of it."

She studied it for a moment and gave it back to Moe. "That's odd. Do you think it might be the Red Sox?"

"I guess it could be, but they could call or put a note with it. They wouldn't just send a ticket. I don't think they would."

She touched the side of his face. "Well, if it is, go see them. You've been moping around here for weeks, and I don't like the looks of what being unemployed is doing to you. Who knows, maybe once the Yankees see you with the competition, they'll make you an offer to come here."

"That's assuming it is from the Sox. I mean, that's quite a stretch."

"What have you got to lose? Take the trip. It'll get you out of the apartment for a while. You like riding the train. Make a day of it.

He tossed the ticket onto the table and said, "It sounds like a come-on to me, but I'll think about it. I could stand a day out of the city."

"Do it. And, while you're there, pick up some chowder."

* * * *

Berg debated about whether to take the train to the point that it almost made him late. He stepped aboard just as it was leaving the station. He climbed the few steps and entered the car to find it empty, save for one man. The man looked up from his seat in the middle of the car and gestured for Moe to come closer. Berg took deliberate steps, shoved the ticket into his pocket, and stooped next to the man. "Wild Bill Donovan. Are you the one who sent the ticket?"

"Please have a seat, Moe. I rented the whole car, so we could talk privately."

The leather seat whispered a puff of air, as he sat. "If the train were not in motion, I would get off. You know that, don't you?"

"Now, you haven't even heard what I have to say. Don't be so rash. If nothing else happens today, you will have a nice lunch and a pleasant ride."

"A nice lunch? Yes. A pleasant ride? That remains to be seen. What do you want with me?"

Donovan motioned for the steward, and he brought them each a cup of coffee before leaving them alone. "I love a good cup of coffee on the train. In the old days, they didn't have bathrooms onboard. You'd have to take a leak off the side of the train, piss flying all over the place. But, those were fun days."

"Yeah, it sounds like it. Come on, Bill, what is it?"

"We need you for a mission and, before you say no, hear me out. When you were interviewing physicists in Italy, what name kept coming up when you asked about the atomic bomb project?"

"Werner Heisenberg. Some of them said he had nothing to do with the project, but I think they were lying. Why would they bother to mention his name, if he weren't involved? And, the others said he was the only one who could pull it off. Heisenberg. He's the guy."

"He is the guy, and he is on his way to Zurich to give a speech."

"I thought they had him under special protection, almost house arrest."

"They have, and that's why we couldn't get at him. We tried bombing his office, but he wasn't there. Now, he's headed for Switzerland. It's the one country the German scientists are permitted to visit."

"Okay, so what has that got to do with me?"

"We want you to go to Zurich, listen to what he has to say and, if it sounds like they're close to perfecting the bomb, kill him."

"Hold the phone. I'm no assassin. I saw enough killing. Besides, you've got plenty of operatives who are very capable of murdering somebody without using me."

"None of them understand physics like you do. I've seen the books in your office. You're the only one who could make an intelligent evaluation of how close the Germans are to completing the project." Moe wagged his head, and Donovan said, "You may not believe this, but we listened when you said we shouldn't be like the Nazis. We don't want to kill the guy unless we have to. If Hitler gets the bomb, he'll overrun every country that gets in his way. There's no restraint with that guy. He'll rid the world of the Jews and every other group he decides doesn't deserve to live. We're talking millions of lives. If Heisenberg is close, we need to deny Germany of his brain. This goes all the way to the top, Moe, to the president."

"You give me too much credit. Quantum mechanics is a complex science, and I'm not a physicist, not by a long shot."

"What do you think of Heisenberg's uncertainty principle?"

"Some say the loss of precision is not as acute as Heisenberg predicts, but the basic principle is still sound. The man is a smart guy. After all, he did win the Nobel Prize."

"There isn't another person in Washington, and certainly not in the OSS, who has even heard of the uncertainty principle. I wouldn't have known to ask about it, if you hadn't underlined that paragraph in one of your books."

"Well, I appreciate your thinking of me, Bill, but my answer has to be no. And, I'm final on that."

"All right. If that's your last word, I respect it." He stared out the window, as he finished his coffee. "I'll be leaving you when we get to Boston."

"I know I shouldn't ask, but do you have business there?"

"I just need to make a phone call."

Moe sat quietly until his imagination took control. "Is your call going to Washington?"

"It is. Moe, this is by far the most critical mission of the war. You would expect us to have a contingency plan for your refusal to help."

"Shit. You want me to think you're going to call someone to go kill Heisenberg, so I'll feel pressured. It won't work. I'm not going. I quit. Can't you understand that?"

"I fully understand it, and I'm not asking you to go. That discussion is over, but our business must go on. We have to assume Heisenberg poses a very real threat to national security, and we'll take care of him, permanently. That's what we do. We're not going to wait for Hitler to build another Auschwitz in London or New Jersey."

"Damn you, Donovan."

* * * *

Stella's words still rang in his mind, as Berg looked out the plane window at the runway in London. "Don't go," she had said. "If they get their hooks back into you, I'll lose you forever. Think of me. Think of the life we can have together, children, growing old." There was no good answer, only an array of bad choices, and he made his. Their happiness and even his own life were nothing compared to what Hitler could do with a super weapon. The plane skidded on the tarmac and taxied to the terminal. An OSS car and driver were waiting for him and took him to the London office.

"Woodrow Treadwell. I thought you'd be gone by now."

"I don't have the option of just quitting, Moe. I signed on to work in Europe for the duration of the war."

"Then you have my sympathy. I am here for one mission. That's it, and then I'm going home. Oh, speaking of home, I gave my girl this address, if she needs to call or write. Keep an eye out for a letter for me, will you? I don't want her to think I've forgotten her."

"Sure, we're not heartless here, no matter what you might think."

"Thanks. So, I'm here. What do you want me to do?"

"Heisenberg's speech is set for two weeks from now. You'll be in London for a time, brushing up with our scientists, so you can pass yourself off as a university student when you get to Zurich. We think it's the best cover. No one will expect you to know everything about physics, if you're a student."

"I'm a little old for a student, but that's okay. I'll come up with a story for that."

"It has been hard for us to admit, but we are not as experienced in these matters as we need to be. We've made mistakes, and people have died because of those mistakes. So, we're partnering with MI6 on this one. You worked with one of their agents in Brazil, and that familiarity might be of value now."

"You're talking about Lydia."

"When the time is right, we'll fly the two of you to Marseille, and from there you'll travel by train to Switzerland. Take rooms at the hotel across the street from the lecture hall." He reached into his desk drawer and took out a pistol and a tablet. "You'll need these."

"Wow. A forty-five caliber and the L pill. You're serious."

"I'm sorry, Moe, but we can't afford to have you captured and tortured. You know too much. If you have to kill Heisenberg, take the pill. It's better than what the Gestapo would do to you."

"I've seen their handy work, and you're right. I'd be better off dead."

Treadwell pressed the call button on his intercom. "Helvi, would you please come in?"

She came through the door standing a full six feet tall, with long, blonde hair and a complexion as fair as he'd ever seen. "I believe he called you Helvi. Is that right?"

"Yes, and I will be your contact while you are in London."

"You don't look very British/"

"I am from Finland, and you, I believe, are the famous baseball player from America."

"I played baseball, but I'm not sure how famous I am."

"You are too modest, and remember, I am OSS. We have our ways of learning about people, even our own people." She gestured toward the open door and said, "Come with me, and I will get you started. We have a lot of work to do. I expect to work with you every day and well into the night. There is nothing I won't do to help you get ready."

"Well, that sounds like a lovely offer. How could any man resist?"

* * * *

The gash on the side of Lydia's head was fully healed when they boarded the train in Marseille. She seemed uneasy, twisting in her seat and fidgeting with something in her purse. "Would you rather have the window seat?" Moe asked.

"No, thank you. I prefer the aisle in the event we have to leave in a hurry." She snapped the purse shut and stuffed it beside her. "How many papers do you have there?"

"Only three. I got two before we left London, and the third is a local. It's interesting to see how different countries spin the details of the same stories. One of the reasons I like to travel by train is that it allows me to read. Cars always seem to be stopping or turning. They're not conducive to someone who likes to read as much as I do."

"I thought you'd be studying a book on physics, making those last minute preparations."

"Reading the same material more than once is of no value to me. I know as much as I'm going to know on that topic. I'd rather spend my time enjoying the ride and the company."

"That's very nice of you, Moe."

"I'm glad it's you. So, tell me, how do you plan to do it?"

"Do what?"

"Kill me."

"What a crazy thing to ask. I'm your friend. I'm here to help you."

"No, you're not. You're here to watch me. There's nothing you can do to help me get into that lecture hall and nothing you can do to help me decide whether to shoot the man. If I don't kill him, I walk out like I came in. If I do kill him, then I take the L pill, and it's all over. Tell me the truth, Lydia. I deserve that much."

She answered in a thoughtful, measured tone. "Yes, you do. MI6 agreed to help under one condition, that we have the assurance that you won't be caught, if you kill Professor Heisenberg. In my luggage is a rifle. I will assemble it on top of one of the buildings. I can't tell you which one, but it will give me full view of the front and side exit doors. Should you come out alone, I will disassemble the rifle and return to my room. If you come out in handcuffs, I am to shoot you dead, and I'm an excellent shot."

"Then that makes you a doubly good choice to accompany me. You don't miss your target, and you know me well enough to win my trust. Well done, MI6."

"I'm sorry, Moe. Of course, you could make things a lot easier for me, if you take the pill once you shoot him."

"I believe I would, but I can't swear to that. It's bad enough to murder a man. Committing suicide is worse. I don't think any of us know whether we'd really do either of those until the time comes. The backup plan makes perfect sense, and you would probably be saving me from a lot of pain."

"I don't take this lightly, Moe, but you can be sure I will do my job."

Chapter Eleven

Moe and Lydia walked through a cloud of steam, as they passed by the engine of the locomotive at the rail station in Zurich. It seemed to foreshadow the haze of uncertainty on the mission and whether one of them would have to kill the other. Berg pulled up the collar of his overcoat to ward off the bitter cold, and he said nothing. What was there to say? He had the rest of the evening and the next day before having to face death, Heisenberg's and perhaps his own. He wondered if he'd see his father in the next life and, if he did, would the old man still be as grumpy as he was in this life? *Chances are you'll go straight to hell, Moe, after murder and suicide. No, don't think like that. The die is cast. Enjoy a nice dinner tonight, sleep late in the morning, and spend the day walking the streets of a city you've never seen. That's the ticket.*

Lydia stepped closer and whispered. "Did you notice the man following us?"

"I guess I was distracted. Let's stop, and I'll tie my shoe. See what he does." Berg knelt, thinking, *I wish my gun was in my belt instead of in the suitcase.* The man walked past without looking at either of them. "Maybe we're just a little paranoid."

"Perhaps, but he was wearing a gray overcoat with white pinstripes, in case we see him again."

They hired a car to take them to the hotel and noticed a set of headlights following fifty yards behind. When they reached the front desk, a man in a gray overcoat eased into the lobby and sat next to the fountain. "Well, Lydia, I believe we have a shadow. Let's get checked in and take our things to the rooms. I'll meet you in the bar in half an hour, and we'll see whether he is still with us."

Berg's room was modest compared to the one he had in Rome, but he had a full view of the lecture hall, and he wondered if it would be the same kind of view Lydia would have with her rifle. The front and side of the hall were both well lighted. She'd have a difficult time missing him. But, he'd worry about that tomorrow night. He took a quick bath and dressed in black pants and white shirt before draping his coat over his arm and heading downstairs. He found Lydia at the bar, already half way through a tall glass of beer. "Did you see our friend?"

"He moved to a chair near the telephone booths. I almost missed him."

"Then let's find out what he's up to. Do you have your pistol?"

"Why do you bother to ask? Of course, I do."

"I'm going to walk outside and then down the alley, while you finish your drink. If he follows, come after us, but be coy about it, keep that gun in your pocket, and don't get involved unless you see my life is in danger. I don't want to tip our hand if this guy is just curious."

"I know what to do, Moe. This isn't my first time dealing with a shadow."

Berg pulled his coat on, as he walked through the lobby and out the door. He paced himself to give the man in the gray coat time to exit the hotel and see him turn into the alley. The narrow passage smelled of urine and rotting food. *Man, it's dark in here. Good place to get your throat cut.* He turned the back corner of the building and stood flat against the wall, holding his breath so as not to make a sound. He waited for what seemed like a long time, and the man passed in front of him. Should he turn the game and be the one who follows? No, he hadn't the patience for that. He grabbed the man's coat and yanked him to the wall. "Who are you, and why are you following me?"

"Oh, I'm not following you."

"No, of course not. You just like walking down dark alleys in the night." Moe lifted him off the ground and jammed him into the wall. "You're going to tell me why you're following me, or I'm going to beat you like a dog."

"Please, please, don't hurt me. I mean you no harm"

Berg pulled him under the light of a single bulb at the kitchen door. "Are you crying?" The man sobbed, Berg let him go, and he stumbled away. "Is that you, Lydia?"

"Yes, I was standing in the dark watching. Did you say he was crying?"

"That's what I said, and agents of the Gestapo don't cry for any reason. I don't know what he wanted, but I'm glad we didn't have to kill him. Finding a stiff in an alley across the street from the lecture hall could bring extra security tomorrow night. Getting in there with a gun is going to be iffy enough without that."

"You shouldn't have let him go. He may not be Gestapo, but that doesn't mean he won't come back and slit your throat in your sleep. We could've taken the body somewhere else to dump it."

"How? In the trunk of a taxi?"

"We have people who take care of those kinds of things. I could have called them from my room, but it doesn't matter now. Thanks to you, we have a man running loose, and we don't know what his interest is in us."

"I'm sorry, Lydia, but I'm not that cold blooded."

"Well, you had better be cold blooded tomorrow night. The outcome of this war could turn on whether you have the nerve to pull the trigger."

* * * *

Berg's plan to sleep late the next morning was thwarted by the knot in his stomach. He breakfasted alone, but his eggs, potatoes, and coffee didn't settle the rumbling inside. He walked for miles, past the Fraumünster Church and by the lake, adorned with reflections of the mountains that rose behind it. And, with every step he prayed the clock would stop, that he would not have to go through with murdering a man he was learning to respect, and that somehow this war would be over. But, the war wasn't over, nor would it be until the question of atomic weapons was answered. If he waited, Hitler would answer it for him. The clock at Saint Peter's Church tolled three o'clock, and Berg turned back for the hotel. There was no escaping his duty.

He dined early and, again, ate alone. A steak cooked rare, oozing with red juices, and a bottle of Cabernet, followed by cherries jubilee and strong coffee. *Well, if I die tonight, at least I'll die well fed. Maybe I don't have to die. How could I shoot him and get away? I don't have to kill him during his speech. Yeah, but you can't afford to miss the chance, Moe. Do what has to be done.* And, so the debate went on inside his head, until it was time to go.

He paid the bill and stepped into the cold streets. The guard at the entrance checked his papers, they exchanged a few words, and Moe Berg the assassin was inside. He handed his overcoat to the girl at the check stand and looked at his ticket. *Number eighty-six. That's fitting.* He almost laughed. Life had become that ridiculous. The sound of his steps seemed to echo in the lecture hall. *My, God*, he thought. *This man can change the course of history, and only twenty people came to hear him. Maybe that's why they let me in.* The aging, wooden seat groaned as he sat, and in a matter of minutes Heisenberg took the stage.

The man was smaller than Berg expected, slightly built, and his mellow voice was barely audible. Moe moved down to the second row and started taking notes. Heisenberg spoke like a scientist, bouncing from one topic to another and fumbling with his stick of chalk every time he wrote on the blackboard. His gaze moved across the room, but kept coming back to Moe. *Why does he keep looking at me? Does he know something? Calm down, Moe. You're the only one taking notes. That's all.* When the speech ended, Heisenberg stood on the stage, greeting the people who came and shaking hands. Was he close to perfecting the bomb? Moe wasn't sure. He went to the end of the line and waited his turn to meet the renowned physicists. "Thank you for sharing your theories with us, Professor Heisenberg. I am a student at the University of Basel and a great admirer of your work."

"Thank you. I noticed your taking notes, and now I understand. Are you working on a paper?"

"I am, but I would've come to see you even if I were not. You are a great scientist, and your theories are undeniable, but I must ask you. Do you believe that man can actually harness the power of the atom without devastating consequences?

"That is one of the great misunderstandings of my work, that the only purpose for developing atomic energy would be for destruction. There are innumerable uses, many we have not begun to explore."

"It sounds like you have made great progress, and I should like to talk with you for hours, but I'll not impose on your time. I suppose I've heard all I need to know for now without being rude."

He slipped his hand inside his jacket to the handle of his pistol, and Heisenberg placed his hand on Berg's arm. "We have never heard enough until we have heard all, young man. Would you join me for a drink?"

"I don't want to impose."

"It is no imposition. I left my wife and children to have dinner at my hotel before coming to the lecture hall. I'd like for you to meet them before they're off to bed." He paused, looked down at Moe's arm, and said, "Come, please. It is but a short distance."

Berg pulled his hand out. "I would be honored, Professor." They walked toward the exit flanked by a German soldier on each side. And, Berg remembered Lydia. *Shit, if I walk out of here like this, she'll think I'm under arrest.* "Professor, do we really need an escort just to have a drink?"

Heisenberg motioned to the soldiers. "Please follow a few steps behind. My friend and I would like to talk."

They reached the sidewalk, and the soldiers were still closer than Berg would've liked. He scanned the rooftops. *I hope she's not as good a shot as she said she is.*

"Is something wrong?" Heisenberg asked.

"No, I just love the beauty of the city so much, even at night. The snow seems to bring everything to life."

"And, I love it as well. It reminds me of my beloved Germany. Our home in Bavaria is much like this in the winter. Ah, here we are. I told you it would be a short walk." The soldiers stopped in the lobby, while Moe and Heisenberg entered the dining room. A middle-aged lady and three children sat at an empty table. Heisenberg kissed each of them and said, "This is my wife, Elisabeth, and these are our children. Are they not lovely?"

"Indeed they are. I am so happy to meet you, Mrs. Heisenberg."

"And, I to meet you, but I must apologize and leave you. I was waiting for the children to see their father before putting them to bed." Her eyes welled, and she said, "Good night, dear sir. I pray your visit goes well. My husband is a good man."

The children rose and each recited, "Good night, father" before following their mother out of the room. The two men sat and ordered wine. Heisenberg took two cigars from his vest pocket. "Would you like a smoke?"

"Thank you, but I don't smoke. But, please, don't let me keep you from enjoying your cigar." Heisenberg lit the cigar and drank down a full glass of wine. "You take your drinking seriously, don't you, Professor?"

"Please call me Werner, and thank you for allowing me a last smoke."

"I'm not sure I understand, but you are welcome."

"I sent my family away so they would not have to witness my execution."

"Execution? Professor, uh, Werner, why do you think someone is going to execute you?"

"Not someone, Mr. Berg, you." He filled another glass and drank it down as quickly as the first. "You would have killed me already, but you weren't sure about it. That tells me you are a man of principle. I would not wish to be assassinated by anyone of lesser character."

"If you know my name, I suppose it would be fruitless for me to deny why I'm here."

"The SS may not know you, but we in the scientific community are not ignorant of the genius baseball player. We hear your radio broadcasts and read your newspapers. I have known you were in the city from the time you arrived."

"So, that was your man who was following me?"

"He should not have pursued you into the alley. That was foolhardy, and he deserved to have you shove him around. Tell me, Moe, how do you plan to carry off your plot?"

Berg sipped his wine and said, "I had intended to shoot you twice in the chest, hoping to hit the heart, so your death would be quick and painless."

"That is quite decent of you."

"Yes, well, I'm not a heartless killer, only a patriot, trying to keep you from developing a monstrous weapon for the Third Reich."

"I am not working on this project for the Reich or for Hitler. I work for Germany and, like you, I am a patriot. But, please go on."

He poured another glass of wine, as Berg answered. "Funny, I had this same conversation with someone on the train coming here. Very well, then. Having shot you, I would turn my weapon on those two soldiers at the table across the room, hoping to kill them both before they kill me. Then I would've walked out the back door and do what I do best."

"And, what do you do best?"

"Blend in, disappear into the streets."

"You said you would've done that. Have your plans changed?"

"The part about walking out the door has changed. I suppose the men in black suits seated behind me are SS, and they would surely kill me before I could escape."

"They follow me everywhere I go."

"So, we have a dilemma, Werner. One patriot trying to kill another, and both die."

"Perhaps I can offer an alternative."

"That would be most appreciated."

"The napkin before you contains the critical information your scientists are missing for creation of the weapon. With it, they will break through in a matter of weeks. I wrote the instructions in Sanskrit, which I know you can translate. In that way, I am assured that only you will deliver the information to your government. In order to take it to them, you must leave here alive, and I can help you with that, but I must have your sworn oath before I do."

"I cannot give my word until I know what you want."

"I told you that I am a loyal German. I have delayed completion of this project as long as I can. If I delay much longer, they will kill one of my children to show their resolve, and they have told me that. I hate the Nazis, but I love Germany. If I share this data with you, you must not give it to your government until they swear it will not be used for an attack on my country."

"Intriguing. So, if it were used on troops in the Philippines or Japan, you'd have no issues with that?"

"I, too, am not a heartless killer, Mr. Berg. Once you have the bomb, I would suggest a very public display, somewhere uninhabited, perhaps in the Sahara. Show the world what you have, and the Fuehrer will come to terms with you. Japan should follow but, if not, my concern is for Germany." He took a long draw on his cigar, let the smoke trickle from his lips, and said, "Do we have an agreement?"

"We do, sir, but you are under close surveillance. How shall I take the napkin without raising suspicion?"

"I have been drinking heavily since we sat. My friends from the SS will report on that, and I shall be sternly warned not to repeat my overindulgence in the future. In a moment I shall spill my glass of wine on you. As you stand, take the napkin and use it to dry your pants and then discretely stuff it into a pocket. Can you do that?"

"I imagine we are about to see. After you, Professor." Moe Berg was slow of foot, but quick of hand. Heisenberg stood, staggered, and tipped his glass over. Moe's well-honed reflexes took over. The SS agents grabbed

Heisenberg before he fell and led him out of the room. Berg took a long drink of wine and whispered, "Good night, Werner, and God bless America."

* * * *

The wind had calmed, but the danger had not. Berg knew he needed to get out of Zurich and do it quickly, before Heisenberg's escorts came looking for him. As he neared his hotel, he saw what he had feared, two men in dark coats, dragging Lydia toward a car. One forced her into the back seat, while the other slid into the driver's seat. She had orders to kill him if captured. Should he kill her? He wrapped his fingers around his pistol and then let it go. *Not yet. You can do better, but do it now.* A swirl of smoke spewed from the exhaust pipe into the cold air, as the engine started. Berg pulled his hat low on his brow and ran toward the car shouting, "Comrade, comrade, stop the car. Professor Heisenberg has been shot." He reached the front door as the driver was opening it. He shoved the man across the bench seat, turned toward the back, and shot the other man three times.

When he pointed the gun at the man on the seat, he begged for his life. "Please, don't kill me. I am a father. I have children." Berg hesitated, but Lydia did not. She grabbed the dead man's pistol, shot the other man, and climbed out of the car.

"Boy that's cold, lady."

"It was necessary. Now, let's get out of here before any more of them come." Moe put his pistol away, and they walked calmly up the sidewalk. "Thank you for the help. I thought I was a dead woman."

"It takes a lot of gall for German agents to arrest somebody in a neutral country."

"That's why they came so late and didn't send uniformed soldiers, so they could blame it on the Russians."

"In a strange way, that makes sense. Heisenberg isn't close on the bomb. He must be five or six years away, so I chose not to kill him."

"I was a little confused when you came out of the building together. I nearly shot both of you. My finger was on the trigger."

"Then I suppose that turned out well for all of us. Here, let's go down this street and get out of sight."

"Good idea, but where are we headed?"

"To the train station."

"That's the last place we want to go. I don't know how many people the Nazis have in town, but you can believe they'll be at the station. No, I say we steal a car and do the best we can."

"And, where would we go, Lydia? North is Germany, west is occupied France, and the other directions aren't much better. We only got in on the train by posing as Swiss nationals, and that won't work once the word is out on us. No, the train is our best chance. Once it gets rolling, they'll have a tough time stopping it."

She walked quietly for the next block and then said, "All right, we'll try it, but how do we deal with the stops along the way. The Germans will radio ahead."

"We'll have to take control of the train and run through those stops. We'll need to restrain the engineer once we get to Marseille, or he'll put the local police on us."

"We could throw him off the train before we get there."

"Wow. Remind me never to make you mad." They circled the depot building, crossed the tracks, and waited behind an empty car until the engineer sounded his whistle. As the train jerked into motion, they sprinted through the snow, bounded onto the steps, and Moe put his gun to the engineer's head. "If you want to live, keep this thing moving and don't stop for anything. And, I mean anything."

* * * *

The train shot through three designated stops and reached Marseille with the engineer neatly bound, gagged, and stuffed under a stack of wood. They wasted no time getting to the landing strip and boarding the plane back to England, and there they parted company with a quick hug and a kiss on the cheek. Berg spent the next two weeks at the OSS office in London, working on the Sanskrit translation. He had finished it the first day, but he delayed until Treadwell brought him word from Washington. "I have two messages for you, Moe. The first is that the Pentagon agrees they will not drop the bomb on Germany. I think the president still wants to get even with Japan over what they did at Pearl."

"Okay, and what's the second part?"

"It's a message from President Roosevelt. He says, 'I hope Heisenberg is right, and my regards to the catcher.' It's not every day you get a personal message from the President of the United States."

"That's nice, especially now. I heard his health is not good."

"I couldn't say. Oh, here. This letter came for you this morning. I've had it in my pocket."

"Thanks, Woodrow. It's from my girl. We're getting married when I get home." Berg stepped aside and opened the envelope.

Dear Moe,

I write to you with heavy heart, but I can't go through this any longer. Charles and I were married this morning, and I'm moving to his home on Staten Island. This was the most difficult decision of my life, but I had to do it before you came back. If I had waited, I couldn't have gone through with it, and I cannot continue to share you with the government. How many times have you promised to give it up? And, you don't. I don't blame you, not really. You don't know how to stop. There is no reason for you to answer this letter and please don't look for me. I will always love you, Moe, but I can't be with you anymore.
   Stella

Moe read the letter three times, and each time ripped at his heart more than the last. He crushed it in his fist and looked at Helvi. "Say, pretty girl, how would you like to have dinner with me? Better yet, would you like to see Paris?"

* * * *

Moe Berg stood gazing out the window at Rue d'Assas and the campus of Sorbonne University. Not much had changed since twenty years ago. Paris had fallen without much resistance, and the German Army had fled from the Allies just as quickly. He thought of those carefree days when he was a student, the days he played baseball for the sheer fun of it. Helvi called to him from the bed. "What are you doing?"

"Just having a coffee and taking in the beauty of the city."

"Have you not seen the city for the six months we've been here?"

"I have, but something is different today." He set his cup down, sat on the edge of the bed, and took her hand.

"It's been good for me to be here with you. You've been a lover unlike any I've known, and you've become a dear friend to me."

"You sound like someone who is about to leave. Don't do that."

"I'm going to New York. I have some unfinished business there, a question I need to ask, and I can never be at peace until I hear the answer."

"It's another woman, isn't it?" He nodded, and she said, "Then go, if you must, but do not come back to me. I will not share you. We can be happy, Moe. Don't do this thing."

"I must."

* * * *

Lady Liberty stood in clear view from the top deck of the Staten Island Ferry, her torch outstretched to cast its light on a world in turmoil. The cool air of autumn filled his lungs, lifting his spirits in a way only New York could do. Berg passed by the grand statue and reached the dock with but one thought in mind. He handed the cabbie a scrap of paper with an address scrawled on it and rode in silence until they stopped by the curb at a white house with green shutters. The taxi pulled away, and Moe stood on the sidewalk, wondering whether this was a mistake. But, it didn't matter now. He was here and he would see it through.

His shoes brushed through neatly trimmed grass, still damp with the morning dew. He knocked three times. A voice from within caught his ear, as the door opened. "Did you forget something, dear?" She was as beautiful as ever. "Oh, my God. Moe, what are you doing here?"

"I'm not here to cause trouble for you. I only wanted to see you once more."

"Well, I'd invite you in, but you know how things are. I mean, how did you find me?"

"I'm a spy, Stella. We know things."

"Then you know I'm married now. He's a good man, Moe. You'd like him."

"Do you love him?"

"You have no right to ask me that."

"Do you love him?"

"I need what he gives me. Stability and knowing he'll be here when I'm lonely."

"Do you still love me?"

"Oh, Moe, please, please don't do this."

"Do you still love me?"

"You're the boy, who never quite grew up, and I love that about you. But, loving you just isn't enough, not anymore."

"It was enough for me." He blew her a kiss and said, "I hope your life is a happy one. I won't bother you again."

"I'm sorry. I wish things could have been different." And, she closed the door.

He shuffled to the end of the sidewalk, thumbs wedged under his belt, and turned to find her watching him from the window. His heart filled with bittersweet memories and the thoughts of what might have been. He gave her a smile and then hailed a taxi. Where would he go now? What would he do with his life? The cab coasted to a stop beside him, he opened the back door, and looked inside to find a man in a tweed suit. "Well, as I live and breathe, Mr. Treadwell. Are you in the taxi business now?"

Treadwell patted the seat and said, "Your country needs you, Moe. Will you help her?"

Moe leaned toward the car, and then he heard the sound of a door opening and Stella's voice calling to him. "Wait. Don't go." She ran down the sidewalk, leapt into his arms, and he held her like never before. "Hold me, Moe, and don't you ever leave me again."

He answered only with his heart, and he turned to Treadwell. "Goodbye, Woodrow. Thanks for the offer, but I don't need a cab anymore."

End

Rudolph Hoss was convicted of war crimes at the Nuremburg trials. When accused of having murdered 3.5 million people at Auschwitz, he answered that he killed only 2.5 million, and the rest died of starvation and disease. He appeared unrepentant until the week before he was hanged, when he called for a priest to take his confession.

Wilhelm Canaris was arrested for his part in a plot to kill Hitler and was put to death on April 9, 1945, just weeks before Hitler's suicide and the end of the war.

Pope Pius XII continued to serve as pope until his death in 1958.

Werner Heisenberg fathered seven children, and he died of cancer in 1972.

When the OSS was dissolved, Moe Berg contracted with the newly-formed CIA. He never learned to drive, he never owned a house, and he never married. He never returned to work in baseball and is the only player to have his baseball card on display at the CIA. Moe died in 1972 following a fall at Ethel's house. He was offered the Medal of Freedom but refused, and it was awarded to him after his death.

This story is a work of fiction, inspired by the life of Moe Berg.

Made in the USA
San Bernardino, CA
15 January 2020

63215651R00117